WHEN I WAS A HORSE

BRIANDA DOMECQ

Translated by Kay (Kayla) S. García

TCU Press *Fort Worth*

Library of Congress Cataloging-in-Publication Data

Domecq, Brianda.
When I was a horse / by Brianda Domecq ; translated by
Kay (Kayla) S. García.
p. cm.
Includes bibliographical references and index.
ISBN-13: 978-0-87565-325-9 (alk. paper)
ISBN-10: 0s-87565-325-1
1. Domecq, Brianda--Translations into English. I. García,
Kay (Kayla) S., 1951- II. Title.
PQ7298.14.O35A24 2006
863'.64--dc22
2005024862

TCU Press
P.O. Box 298300
Fort Worth, Texas 76129
817-257-7822
http://www.prs.tcu.edu
To order books: 1-800-826-8911

Printed in Canada

Cover illustration and design by
Barbara Mathews Whitehead

CONTENTS

PREFACE

Mexican women's imaginations and lives have been limited for centuries by the traditional division between the Virgin of Guadalupe, who represents the virtuous, submissive woman, and the Malinche, who symbolizes the treacherous whore. The female characters of most Mexican writers either conform to these archetypes or succumb to prostitution, insanity, imprisonment, immobilization (being turned into a rock, or a mannequin), or death. However, in the past three decades, a few Mexican women writers have begun to depict a new kind of female protagonist, one that defies society's dictums and forges her own destiny. Ethel Krause, Inés Arredondo, and María Luisa Mendoza have published short stories with strong, rebellious female characters. Elena Poniatowska, Silvia Molina, Angeles Mastretta, and Brianda Domecq have all published short stories and novels with unusually powerful protagonists. I have written extensively on the latter four authors in my work *Broken Bars: New Perspectives from Mexican Women Writers* (1994). Since then, Carmen Boullosa has published *Treinta Años* (1999) (published in English as *Leaving Tabasco*), the main character of which escapes from a suffocating home environment and a dangerously oppressive political regime and makes a new life for herself.

The literary presentation of emancipatory alternatives for women, a theme that is present in many of Brianda Domecq's stories included in this volume, reflects the changing reality of Mexican society. In the past few decades, increasing numbers of women have entered the professional workforce, becoming doctors, lawyers, professors, engineers, or scientists, but their achievements are often ignored by the mass media and by writers who focus more on what needs to be changed than on what is actually changing. Although the value of sociopolitical protest is evident in Latin America, there is also a need for inspiration. The abovementioned authors are providing a service by presenting women in a positive way in their works, and by becoming role models in their own right. They have juggled the roles of wife, mother, breadwinner, and writer, and they tell their stories from the point of view of a woman, based on the personal experience that only a woman can have. Not only do their lives shape and inform their writing, but their literary works also influence their lives, and a recognition of this interaction is essential to the understanding of their texts. For this reason I have included information on both Brianda Domecq's life and her work in the introduction to this volume and her autobiography at the end of this book, as one last story, or the master story from which all others are derived. In the introduction, my words are interwoven with Brianda's, creating a dialogue that includes the reader and invites him/her to participate in the process of discovery.

THE JOURNEY TOWARD FREEDOM:

AN INTRODUCTION TO BRIANDA DOMECQ

by Kay (Kayla) S. García

*We are beginning to acquire the habit of freedom: external freedom to move in the world, internal freedom to know ourselves and to reveal ourselves as we are, the freedom to live in service to ourselves and not in service to others.** In the past several years the Mexican novelist, Brianda Domecq, has liberated herself in succession from alcohol, nicotine, and a codependent marriage. For her, moving toward freedom has been a slow, excruciatingly painful growth process, which she mapped out for herself in her writing as a preamble to real life. The first step was finding courage, *the courage to say what we think and to accept the consequences; the courage to confront the unavoidable solitude that results when a woman acts and speaks with sincerity in this society that is still patriarchal; the courage*

*Brianda's words in italics are taken from her published works (listed in the Bibliography at the end of the book) as well as from an interview that I did with her in July 1993.

to confront reality directly, in spite of the masculine figures that guard the doors of our lives (father, brother, husband, son, priest).

Brianda's personal journey began in earnest when she closed the door on a whole period of her life: her existence as housekeeper, wife, and mother. Her daughter was already married, so when her son married also, she felt a tremendous weight being lifted from her shoulders . . . *and now it was time for me to be ME. And this search has led me through very painful transformations, as I face problems in my life and grow through them and out of them into a new being, trying to create that center, the core, that it is so difficult for women to develop because we learn to live for others and through others. Seldom do we discover how to evolve through our inner self first and then out towards others. And this has been part of my transformation. I have moved away from things that were distracting me or covering up my true being, my true emotions—things like alcohol, cigarettes, and a worn out, dependent relationship—and have begun to look for myself, to look at myself, working through the pain of growth and discovery, which although unpleasant, will always lead to something more than what avoidance would.*

Brianda was born in 1942 in New York City to Pedro Domecq, the well-known wine producer, and Elizabeth Cook, a beautiful model from New York. When Brianda was nine years old they moved to Mexico City, where a new language and culture exacerbated Brianda's pre-adolescent rebelliousness. For years she bounced back and forth between the two countries, until she finally settled in Mexico and assumed her present identity as a Mexican writer. Although she is completely bilingual, her professional writing is in Spanish, and she is included in the dictionary of Mexican authors published by the national university.

Brianda received a degree in Hispanic language and literature from the Autonomous National University of Mexico

(UNAM) and did one year of graduate study at the prestigious *Colegio de México* in Mexico City. She was editor-in-chief of the *Revista de Bellas Artes* in 1973, and from 1983 to 1985 she was president of PRONATURA, a Mexican conservation association. Because of her economic independence and the fact that her two children are adults, she now has the luxury of being a full-time writer and editor, but that has not always been the case. She and her former husband lived for a long time on his income as a radiologist, and Brianda spent years working as a translator and publicist.

In October of 1978 Brianda was kidnapped by a group of hoodlums who hoped to reap their fortune at her father's expense. *Just a few seconds before, I'd been happily on my way to lunch, knotting some minute threads of my life into problems, but definitely in control of everything, with a normal past, present, and future whose existence gave no signs of coming to an abrupt halt, and then suddenly, reality was something else: a gun, a switchblade, two men and this god-awful, trembling blob of fear sitting in my place. Time had stopped, and what must have been no more than an instant, hung suspended, isolated, unending and incomprehensible. It lasted no longer than the time I took to change seats, less than a lizard needs to lose its tail, only I was the tail, dismembered and seized with absurd, involuntary movements.*

Blindfolded, locked up in a small room with boarded windows, separated from everybody and everything she loved, Brianda had to come to terms with her own human essence. She could still eat, sleep, use the bathroom, listen to the radio, and talk with her captors. She had to comprehend what she could or could not change, to evaluate what freedom she did or did not have, and to face the possibility of imminent death. She chose as her principal survival tactic to reach out to her kidnappers and make them see her as a person, not simply as a victim. One of her greatest challenges was holding on to her own identity and not sinking into a whirlpool of fear, depression, and anxiety. Brianda fictionalized this experience in *Once días . . . y algo más (Eleven Days)*. Leo, the protagonist, is quite closely identified with the author, and the narrative adheres closely to actual events.

Leo makes up humorous names for her captors, plays dominos and Blind Woman's Bluff with them, tells jokes, exchanges recipes, discusses music, listens to their life stories, and gives them advice. Her playfulness disarms the criminals and draws them into a symbiotic relationship with her. *My guard would like to ignore me, but like a moth around a light bulb, he can't distance himself for very long. He doesn't understand my game. Instead of scorn and rejection, acceptance and admiration; instead of rage and resistance, accommodation and jokes. I feel his confusion. He knows that I am playing, but he has doubts, because this isn't the game he expected.*

Leo's strategies help her survive until she is rescued, but once physically released, she faces a long struggle to become psychologically free again, a struggle she calls "the journey back." *Every day, like a painful rite of purification, as if she were washing away a guilt way beyond her comprehension, the tears welled up from that hard, resolute sorrow that had lodged between her stomach and her lungs. Nothing seemed the same. She shut herself in, like someone who has journeyed to the other side of death and doesn't wish to return. Her head was full of voices and footsteps, her skin icy with murmurs and sudden fears . . . Little by little she began to understand.*

In 1982 Brianda published a collection of short stories, *Bestiario doméstico (Domestic Bestiary)*, which deal with the internal and external conflicts faced by women as they pursue their own freedom. All of those stories are included in the present volume, as well as some more recent works. One of

Brianda's quandaries, the obstacle presented by her prestigious last name, is dealt with in humorous fashion in the story "Mr. **Clunk!**" *i live behind, below, and a little to the left of my name . . . i carry my name on my back, and believe me, it's heavy. It's one of those names—it doesn't matter which one—that go "clunk!" when dropped, as if by chance, in the middle of a party.* The protagonist of the story contemplates an ironic rebellion against the burdensome name. *One of these days, as soon as i get up my courage, i'll leave the accursed name hanging there on the door, and escape out the window. Then we'll see what the damn fool does without me.* Although Brianda has not abandoned her father's last name, she has managed to give it new meaning in literary circles.

Another story in the collection, "The Eternal Theater," uses the theater-as-life theme to dramatize the never-ending trap of being wife/housekeeper/mother (and eventually grandmother). Beatrice, the protagonist, aspires to be more than her mother was, so she chooses acting instead of marriage. *That's why I said **no** to Robert—and don't cry Mama—and I'll say **no** to John, Peter, Thomas, or Reuben. Because I'm going to be an actress.*

The brief story "Galatea" deftly illustrates the conflict between a female's nesting instinct and her desire for independence. Another ironic tale, "Adelaide's Body," reveals the futility of aspiring to be male in order to experience freedom and the joy of laying carpets or pretty young maidens.

An extensive section of this collection is a trilogy of stories about Lillith, Adam's first wife who was exiled from Eden for rebelling and refusing to be taken in the missionary position. Although Lillith is mentioned briefly in the Bible as a hoot owl, her real story has been banned from traditional Christianity by historians and theologians, so Brianda has rewritten and expanded upon it. The consequences of her rebellion have been felt not only by Lillith but by all of her descendants. *The story of Lillith and Sammäel is extremely autobiographical. I think all literature is, basically, because if you are to touch others you have to touch yourself first, you have to write from that deep feeling, that deep essence that is part of your life's experience and is accumulated through living and through knowing, through living a conscious life, which is very important.*

Another story, perhaps autobiographical in a prophetic sense, is "Mozart Day," the tale of Mariana, who one day realizes that there is a whole new world outside her perfect, isolated home.

In 1987 Brianda was commissioned to write a book-length essay on the Rio Grande (called the Río Bravo in Mexico) to accompany a collection of photographs. In order to research her project, Brianda took a two-week camping and rafting trip down the river. The result, *Voces y rostros del Bravo (Voices and Faces of the Rio Grande)* is a beautiful tribute to a river and a way of life that developed around it, as well as to the extraordinary freedom of movement that Brianda enjoyed while writing the essay. It is not common for married Mexican women to have such adventures away from home and family.

Brianda's next project, *Acechando al unicornio (Stalking the Unicorn),* 1988, is an anthology of short stories and excerpts from longer works that deal with the theme of virginity. As a literary history, it shows the transformation of literature through time. *But what is more important is how it shows the changing attitudes toward feminine sexuality in different periods. It is good to know where we are coming from in order to have a vision of where we want to go. In this sense, I am not propagating sexist ideas: On the contrary, I am putting them in historical perspective so that they can be seen for what they are.* *Acechando al unicornio* includes some gruesome stories about the tremendous price women have paid for losing their virginity, as well as some more modern stories that challenge the importance of virginity, such as Patricia Gómez Maganda's "De manera que nunca fui virgen" "So I Never Was a Virgin" and Brianda's own story "In Memoriam." This latter story, which is also included in the present volume, presents a young woman who is disillusioned by the inconsequential nature of the act of losing her virginity.

Acechando al unicornio chronicles not only women's servitude to male models of sexuality, but also women's desire to free themselves from stereotypes and from expectations imposed upon them by society. In the stories mentioned, the loss of virginity is seen as a form of liberation, and represents one more step away from restricted lives and toward independent thinking and living. Thus, Brianda has taken a subject that is traditionally taboo, a subject used to manipulate women's thoughts and control their actions, and infused it with a new feminist spirit.

Brianda's second novel, *La insólita historia de la Santa de Cabora (The Astonishing Story of the Saint of Cabora),* is the fictionalized account of a real-life faithhealer, Teresa Urrea (also referred to as Teresita), the illegitimate daughter of a wealthy *hacendado* and of a poor woman who works on his land. Teresita manages to teach herself how to read and write and to become accepted in the home of her father, thus freeing herself from poverty and the limited choices it implies. Because of her unusual healing powers, she becomes known as the Saint of Cabora. Her popularity and her belief in social reform attract the attention of the dictator Porfirio Díaz, eventually leading to her exile. Although the plot seems alien to Brianda's own life, psychologically this work is actually autobiographical. *I was writing Teresita's story, and thought I had gone so deeply into her life that to a certain extent she was writing through me. Now with this process I'm going through, I've gone back and read enormous parts of the novel and realized that they were preambling this process of growth that I am now undergoing. In other words my own unconscious was speaking through Teresita, or she was speaking through my own unconscious and directing me.*

The therapeutic function of literature is obvious in Brianda's work. *So experience that is reflected in literature can be very healing to a person who is moving through a growth period, and it can be very healing for the author, too, because as you write you are projecting a lot of unconscious pain into a character; this pain takes on new meaning as it becomes meaningful for others, so it has a purpose: It becomes transcendent pain.* Part of the therapeutic function is assessing the meaning of Teresita's life. In traditional, patriarchal terms, she could be considered a failure since she was exiled and thus separated from everything that was hers. *Nonetheless, from an existential point of view I believe Teresa succeeded because she was capable of progressively understanding the meaning of her life, of growing with her experiences, and of becoming more and more complete as a human being. She achieved her goal of living in Cabora, accepted her powers and tried to understand them, learned about the role she could or could not have in history, took risks, and made a commitment. I think her life was a success, as a human being, and as an individual. The book ends with death, just as life does, but nevertheless there is something very heroic about Teresa and I don't feel that she is a failure.*

Teresita's life foreshadows Brianda's own struggles for independence and self-knowledge. In the novel, Teresa grapples with the ineffable quality of magic, life, and death as she tries to feel or intuit knowledge rather than analyze it with words. *Understanding that didn't mean repeating it with words, but rather, seeing it: It was the secret of healing, the secret of life and death. She learned to look behind the names of things, to look for the threads that joined them with the rest of life, and discover hidden meanings in order to turn around the intellect, evade reason, free herself from language, and see that indivisible flowing that was, according to her teacher, the true reality.*

Something that is not openly stated in the novel is Teresa's function as a role model. She has obviously served as an inspiration for Brianda, and she could do the same for readers who are embarking upon a similar quest. *I think that any woman who has struggled and who has conquered to some extent her own life and her own understanding of life is a possible role model. Maybe we're seeing new role models for society as a whole, instead of Schwarzenegger and Rambo—the blood-and gore-heroes—we are coming from another point in time and space and creating new possibilities for human development.*

Brianda's subsequent work is a collection of literary essays that she wrote about Mexican women writers, called *Mujer que publica, mujer pública (Woman Who Publishes, Public Woman),* a title that refers to a Mexican saying that equates women writers with prostitutes. The essays chronicle the authors' struggles to free themselves from masculine literary canons and to form their own tradition. *One of the basic problems facing Mexican women writers right now is the lack of serious studies of their work that will situate them not necessarily within the corpus of male literature but within their own tradition, which would give them not only a context but also a vision of evolution. This is what I try to do when I write academic studies of women's works like my essays on Ethel Krause and Inés Arredondo. In the other essays in this collection, the ones you would call nonconventional essays, I'm deconstructing the traditional view of things. I'm deconstructing what exists so as to be able to construct something new.*

Brianda identifies as a psychological barrier the need for validation within a patriarchal society, the fear of not being accepted, which could impede authenticity in women's writing. *It is a challenge to step into your own shoes and talk from your center, but I do believe women are getting there. Texts are becoming more and more honest. This is one of the reasons why I find Ethel Krause's work so tremendously important. She says things that are very uncomfortable, for readers of both sexes, but she does say them, and she says them from her center, and she is extremely critical. Her literature is very painfully deconstructing. She does not use much humor, but rather finds the wound and sort of wiggles the knife around in it.*

In 2000, Brianda published *Un día fui caballo (When I Was a Horse)*, a collection of short stories, several of which appear in this volume. "Of Cheese and Christ" deals with a woman's relationship with her mother, and includes elements of magic realism. "Earl" is the chronicle of a young girl's first love, "The Turtle" depicts the devastation wreaked by poverty and man's indifference to nature, and "Gift of the Jaguar" reveals how indigenous spiritual beliefs can nurture modern Mexican women and contribute to their growth process. The story "When I Was a Horse" shows how a young girl's imagination can nurture and inspire her.

As Brianda continues on her personal journey, she is gradually freeing herself from all kinds of dependencies that were perhaps inhibiting her self-expression. *I don't think I could write my next book without having gone through this process, I mean the book that I have in mind, which is going to follow five or six generations of women through a process of growth and evolution. If I were not getting to the place where I feel I am now, in contact with myself, I wouldn't have known where that evolution was going, so I wouldn't have known why I was writing the book.* Brianda plans to have the family originate in the United States and then migrate to Mexico, as she did, and thus she will be dealing with trans-cultural issues. She will use the women's movement as a backdrop for the novel, reflecting the changes that feminism has effected in society and in individuals' lives. The steps the first woman in this genealogy takes will be part of the last woman's life. *I feel we are all made up of fragments and part of our life journey is to integrate these fragments and then add our own piece. I am pieces of all these women that have preceded me and as I understand them and rewrite their lives, I will be integrating their lives into mine, and then I will add another piece on, which will be my piece.*

As Brianda continues to forge her part, I struggle to extract my own piece from hers. I have lived through her struggles in person and through reading, and I have found my experiences reflected in and shaped by her work. In the summer of 1993, I was recovering from a personal trauma when I traveled to Mexico City with half the manuscript of *Eleven Days* in my suitcase. When she picked me up at the airport, Brianda announced that she was separating from her husband; he hadn't left yet, but I could stay with her in her half of the house. In the battleground that was her home, we completed and re-worked the manuscript as we re-constructed our lives, merging the therapeutic and creative processes in such a way that the boundaries between author and translator, protagonist and reader, and therapist and friend all became blurred. During the day, I rewrote and relived Brianda's ordeal as a kidnap victim sixteen years in the past; during the evenings, I shared her present-day crisis: the dissolution of her marriage to an alcoholic, something I had experienced several years before. Consequently, my identity became all entangled with hers. The result was a better translation, of course, but then I needed to take a solitary trip through the Mexican countryside in order to redefine my boundaries, to figure out where Brianda ended and I began, what was her ordeal, and what was mine, how much I had actually lived through and how much I had projected myself into Brianda's story. As I waited for the bus, my friend fretted and wanted to take me on my journey. "Brianda, you can't take me where I'm going. I have to go by myself." So I took a bus, and another, and another, and finally found my way to a tiny hotel room in a muddy little town, surrounded by the sounds of firecrackers, two bands out of tune, screaming children, slamming doors, and barking dogs. Exasperated, I looked toward the sky and exclaimed, "I've come all this way to meditate. Couldn't it be a little *quieter?*" About sixty seconds later there was an enormous clap of thunder, and a torrential rain began to fall. The firecrackers, bands, children, doors, and dogs all fell silent. Lulled by the pounding water on the low, metal roof of my room, I managed to relocate the solid core at the center of my being and thus was able to write this essay for you, the reader, who represents one more point along the spiral of meaning generated by Brianda's work and life.

WHEN
I
WAS
A
HORSE

MR. CLUNK!

i live behind, below, and a little to the left of my name. That may sound strange because most people *are* their names, and when i say "names" i mean their first and last names. You know what i'm talking about, the label they give us at birth, with which we spend the rest of our lives entering and leaving places—rooms, homes, and dreams—until we die. "Hi, I'm Pepe Pérez," or "Ralph Rodríguez, at your service," or "Here lies Robert Rankin, 1819-1864." That's normal; you carry your name inside, perfectly accommodated to your "I am i." on the other hand, carry my name on my back, and believe me, it's heavy.

It's one of those names—it doesn't matter which— that go **clunk!** when dropped, as if by chance, in the middle of a party or in the office of some civil servant. Names like Rockefeller or Jefferson or Johnnie Walker or Braniff, you understand? One of those names that always march right out in front, leaving the person a bit, or a lot, behind. There's no problem if you are born with an ordinary name and then with a lifetime of effort you make it go **clunk!** But it's lousy when you're just born and they brand you with a **clunk!** only because it's the law.

As a child, i wasn't aware of the problem. My name was used like anybody else's: to scold me, congratulate me, call me, send me to bed, or order me to eat the last bite of eggplant. But that's because a child only has a first name, which grows along with him, so J.J. one year is Joey the next and then Joseph, until he starts grade school and then suddenly he's Joseph-Allen-Lundquist-the-Third-at-your-service, and if the poor kid can't make the leap and catch up to his name, he's screwed!

i was in fourth or fifth grade when it began to dawn on me that my name was several sizes too big for me, like an expensive suit with sleeves too long and shoulders too wide. i was a little short for my age therefore i sat in the first row, but my name always managed to sit right in front of me like a mannequin, so the teacher never saw the real me. When i thought i knew the answer to some question, i would jump up and down in my seat, waving my hand in the air until the teacher turned in my direction.

"Ah! Young Mr. **Clunk!** seems to know the answer," he would say so formally that i would look around to see who he was talking about. He called the other boys "John" or "Pete" or "the kid with long hair." By the time i realized that i was supposed to answer, i had forgotten the question. That's why i never did well in school. But it amused me to look through the eyes of my name, as if it were a mask, and observe how everybody, even the principal, was impressed when they saw it written on my paper.

Adolescence was a different story. You know how one gets during that period: endlessly delving inward, looking for one's identity as if beneath all the confusion one could find a secret key to one's self. And adults don't help at all, always pulling you back out and pressuring you with admonitions like "you have to make up your mind" and "it's time for you to choose your path" and "decide who you are!" Well, nobody was forcing me to decide or choose because everyone seemed to know who i was and where i was going, as if my name were a straight road to Success. That was when my name began to harden around me like a shell, and i was rolled up inside, bouncing around with the questions nobody asked me: Who am i? Where am i going? What am i going to do? And as i searched inside, "Mr. **Clunk!**" became a convenient cover-up. It was a disguise and a shield; i pushed it along in front of me, forcing a cynical little smile, and it opened doors wherever i went.

During the last semester of prep school i won a poetry contest in a magazine. Nobody told me; i read it in the newspaper. i was waiting for somebody to call me but that never happened. Later i discovered that they had published my poems in a magazine with a biographical note about the poet. That really made me mad, so i called the editor to complain about their making up a life for me. He begged my forgiveness and assured me that he had truly believed that Mr. **Clunk!** did not exist, that it was just a pseudonym. Maybe i am the one who doesn't exist, because the name definitely does. i see it every day on billboards, on television, i hear it on the radio, and it's almost always in the newspapers. Besides, i take it everywhere i go. How could it not exist? Complete strangers nod their heads when they hear it and say, "Oh, yes. We know who he is." If that's true, they're doing better than i am.

Actually, i don't really take the name anywhere: It takes me. It leads me back and forth, over here and over there, as if i were a dog on a leash. There goes the name, erect and proud, sure of itself, distinguished, rich, and famous. And i follow behind, wagging my tail to get attention, hoping someone will notice me and scratch my ears or admire my intelligence when i offer my paw to shake. But it never happens. On the street, in meetings, in restaurants, everybody stops when they see the name, they speak to it, ask favors of it, offer business deals to it, send greetings to its father, hint that they should do lunch some day, and then go away feeling honored because they talked to it.

Sometimes i wish i were a real dog so i could pee on their polyester pants.

When i finished prep school, my father wanted me to honor the family name by studying business administration in a private university, but i was adamant about going to a public institution to study literature. There, among the common people, i can be myself, i thought. i still had romantic illusions. Because of my name i had to allow two burly bodyguards to follow me around, but i insisted on entering class alone, hoping i could leave my name out in the hall with the two gorillas.

"Pay no attention to my name," i'd say. "Really, i'm different. i think like you do."

Ha! As soon as i said it i realized that nobody would believe me. How could they? My name is as tall as a skyscraper on Wall Street! That's why i was always tired, from carrying the accursed thing around with me. The myth of Mr. **Clunk!** amidst the "common folk" ended up destroying my own myth of the "common folk" and all my romantic notions of equality. Those revolutionary ideas just covered up the majority's desire to have a name that goes **Clunk!** Hell! They can have mine.

A few months before graduation i met Donna Dumpworth. She was a year behind me but since i had to repeat linguistics, we were in that class together. She was one of the "crowd:" you know, middle-middle-class or lower-middle-class, it's hard to tell because from up here where we **Clunks!** are isolated, they all look the same, like the Chinese. She had black hair and olive skin and she was a little short, which suited me just fine. The only thing that revealed a possible dalliance in her genealogy was the emerald-green of her eyes, but i wasn't about to investigate. She was a true activist, always marching, protesting, demonstrating, picketing, or performing some kind of civil disobedience. Several times i saw her holding a microphone and her voice reached me over the loudspeakers in the main hallway. It would never have occurred to me to approach her, even though i remember a wet dream i had while savoring the smooth way her lips pronounced the word "equality," drawing out the sounds in a tantalizing way: **equaaalllity**, or something like that. So i was surprised the day she came to sit by me.

"Hey, you're cool, you know that?"

i looked around but nobody else was there.

"No! I'm talking to you, silly," she said, laughing. "Really, you must be really far out to come to this university, burdened with a name like yours. I mean it."

Those were her words: "burdened with a name like yours," as if she had seen through my name and she were talking to **me**. i don't know if that is love, but i instantly grew two feet; i grabbed the damn name and stuffed it in my pocket.

"I just don't pay any attention to it," I said. "People can think whatever they wish. I am my own person."

That's how I said it, with a capital letter and everything, and it felt so good that I believed it. Donna abandoned the picket lines and I evaded the gorillas and we began a hot-as-a-chili-pepper romance in the back seat of my car and the front table of expensive restaurants. The back seat was by mutual consent; the front table was because of my name. You can't go anywhere without a reservation. Once we were engaged, Donna lost her voice, that sensuous elongation of *equaaalllity* and the rotundness of her *-isms*—socialism, communism, and of course, egalitarianism—but I didn't notice much because I had found my own, previously muffled voice that for the first time seemed to discover how to say "I am," "I think," "I believe," and even "I want." I was happy to have someone who would listen to **me**. She would open those big green eyes wide and sip her champagne that always appeared magically on the table and on the bill, while I spoke of returning to the simple life, the beauty of the countryside, the search for truth and other romantic ideas that I had gleaned from fiction because I couldn't have found them in my reality. And I would savor my secret plan of our becoming Mr. and Mrs. Dumpworth and leaving the **Clunk!** behind, where it belonged. It wasn't until one week before the wedding that I discovered the engraved letterhead (Mr. and Mrs. **Clunk!**) and the gold-plated plaque (The **Clunks!**) that Donna had ordered for our front door to surprise me.

"I'm just so proud that you would give me your name," she explained. "I can't wait to be introduced as Mrs. **Clunk!**"

Days later, Donna took my name in a ceremony with all due pomp and circumstance, and i went to look for work to support them as well as i could.

For a while i walked around again with my name out in front, checking out the possibility of doing something for myself, a job that would help me recognize who i was. Every door i tried opened wide, all the way to the CEO's office, complete with courtesies and cigars that i inserted in my suit pocket with a flourish only to dump them in the garbage can on my way out. i didn't get any work, but i learned what it means to have a sense of humor. i would start out by announcing my desire to work and my willingness to begin at the bottom.

"God forbid! Ha, ha! What a sense of humor you have! The only position you could fill in this place is mine. Ha, ha! As soon as it's available, I'll tell my widow to let you know."

"I get it! Your old man sent you to drive us to bankruptcy

with the salary we'd have to pay you. Well, he's not going to get away with it. Ha, ha! Say hi to the old fox for me and tell him I wasn't born yesterday. My God! What a sense of humor he has!"

With all that going on, and Donna trotting our name around like a thoroughbred training for the Triple Crown, and a baby **Clunk!** on the way, i had to admit defeat. i didn't find work, but i did get a beautiful office on the fifteenth floor of "**Clunk!** & **Clunk!** Associates." They upholstered all the furniture with fine leather, provided me with a secretary who could be a centerfold for Playboy magazine, and assigned me a monthly salary with six big figures. Everybody knows that i don't do anything, but with my name, who needs to work?

The name, of course, is outside on the door, standing guard: It doesn't want me to tarnish it. i pass the time behind an enormous desk. Sometimes i get under it just to see how that feels, and i even crawl around a little, because nobody ever comes in here. i scribble or make fanciful doodles on the embossed letterhead, lost in fantasies of escape or making up fictitious lives for myself in unknown places, with false names. One of these days, as soon as i get up my courage, i'll leave the accursed name hanging there on the door and without thinking twice, leap out the window. Then we'll see what the damn fool does without me.

THE ETERNAL THEATER

A woman, said Beatrice, while her mother gave her that I-don't-understand-the-younger-generation look. A woman has to choose, while a man can enjoy both family and profession. It's a simple question of mathematics: The hours of the day, minus the hours devoted to a serious profession, minus the hours spent running a home, minus the hours for eating, minus the hours for sleeping, leaves us with approximately minus twenty-four. There aren't enough hours in the day, so we have to choose; it's as simple as that. Understand?

That's why I said no to Robert—and don't cry, Mama—and I'll say no to John, Peter, Thomas, or Reuben. Because I'm going to be an actress. That's my profession, my vocation, like yours was being a housewife and mother for so many years, said Beatrice. (But what lack of imagination, Mama, was what she didn't say.)

And don't worry, I'm not going to miss out on anything. Quite the contrary, said Beatrice, facing her mother's baffled and disheartened look. I'll just avoid the vicious circle of getting married to have a daughter who gets married to have a daughter who gets married. . .and always with the nagging suspicion that maybe it wasn't worth it—and don't look at me like that. I don't mean it as criticism, I just want you to understand that I am different from you: I'm looking for something *more.*

Besides, don't think I've chosen the easy way, said Beatrice to the reflection of her mother in the mirror as she carefully applied eyeliner to her eyelids. The theater world is a constant challenge; every day you have to do better than the day before in order to compete for the good roles. So if you think about it, I've had incredible luck getting a leading part right off the bat, was what Beatrice said to her mother's image in the mirror. (Even though it's in a third-rate theater, was what she didn't say.) I know that the Third World Theater is not exactly right off Broadway, confessed Beatrice, but the play is good and innovative, and it will surely get rave reviews when the critics start coming to see it, she said as she penciled in her eyebrows.

The play is based on the concept of collective catharsis, she said to her mother's don't-speak-to-me-in-Greek face. The director, who spent many years in psychoanalysis for couples, wants to apply those theories on stage to reach a wider audience and make them aware of the need to analyze and transform their own relationships. The plot deals with many aspects of living together. There are five of us in the cast: I am the young wife and mother, Phillip is my husband, and Isabel, who is four years old, plays the part of my daughter. For balance there is a mature couple (to not call them old fogies) who come to visit. Of course, conflicts arise between the two couples because each represents a different generation. Well, you'll see it on opening night, said Beatrice, smiling without crinkling her eyes. The plot is structured but almost all the dialogues are improvised. The director wants us to "live" the roles so that we can communicate directly to the public. It will be a "living play," revealing something new each night within the basic plot. So if it strikes the right chord it could be a great success, don't you think? And if not, well there always will be other plays, other roles. . .I'm still young and I have a lot of years ahead of me. If this play doesn't make it. . .

But the play did make it, it was such a tremendous success on opening night that the thin walls of the Third World Theater shook with the audience's thunderous applause and in the neighboring houses people thought it must be an earthquake. Afterwards, in her dressing room, Beatrice took her embroidered handkerchief out of her pocket and handed it to her mother.

Don't cry, Mama, she said, as she wiped off her make-up and glanced at her mother's image in the mirror, all shriveled up and seized by tremors as if she had hiccups. It's the beginning of a new life for me, don't you feel it? Tonight all the doors of the world opened, and I feel truly fulfilled for the first time. There's no reason to cry. (Unless you're envious because you never threw yourself into the ring, was what she didn't say.)

The director's expectations were minuscule compared to what actually has happened. With the profits from these six months we've renovated the Third World Theater, and I was able to buy a new car and redecorate my apartment. Isn't it marvelous, Mama? exclaimed Beatrice. (Although it must be hard for you to understand what it feels like to be financially independent, was what she thought.)

It's the success of the year, said Beatrice as she studied her eyes in the mirror. The play's been running for twelve months, Mama! I'm sure you realize that this assures me of more important roles, she said, covering up the circles under her eyes with a thin layer of make-up. (I hope I won't be typecast from now on, was what she didn't say.)

We knew the play would be a success, but we never imagined this, sighed Beatrice, shaking her head without losing the rhythm of her facial exercises. Four years, eight months! And the tickets are sold out two years in advance. I know people who have seen it ten or fifteen times and every six months we have a special showing for the critics so they can comment on new developments in the play in their reviews. As the director says, we all have matured with our roles. Really, Mama, do you think these exercises do any good? I mean, a young, twenty-six-year-old woman with a four-year-old daughter is not the same as a thirty-year-old woman with. . .I can't believe Isabel is already eight years old! The situation changes. Besides, this way I can avoid stagnating in a fixed role. I've passed through all possible states of mind and emotion and all the experiences of my character, said Beatrice. (And I'm beginning to feel like it's all part of the same old routine, was what she didn't say.)

But Mama, I'm surprised at you, said Beatrice, lengthening her eye shadow to cover up some new wrinkles. How can you be scandalized by a woman of my age having a lover? Besides, it's not like he's some stranger. Phillip and I have worked together for so many years that I've lost count. It's perfectly natural for us to spend weekends together, too, said Beatrice, massaging the lines around her mouth. Be a love and pass me that cream over there: They say it's marvelous for smoothing out dry skin. Thanks. Besides the fact is that I have physical and emotional needs, and it's not like I'm going to bed with just anybody. But, you know what? Sometimes I think Phillip takes his role too seriously. He gets jealous if I look at another man! And don't worry about Isabel. She's a big girl now and it's time for her to face reality, she said. (And stop making a fuss over Phillip between acts, was what she didn't say.)

You're absolutely right, Mama—left, right, up, down—she panted as she did her calisthenics. I've been thinking about that for some time now but I haven't said anything because I didn't want to hurt her feelings—left, right, up, down. Soon we'll have to replace Isabel—left, right, up, down. Why are you smiling? I mean, it's not good for me to be on stage with a twenty-year-old daughter; I need a younger girl, said Beatrice. (Besides, Isabel is beginning to irritate me; she's aggressive and ambitious, and I think she's after my role, was what she didn't say.)

It's true, Mama, said Beatrice, drying her tears, it's true that for some time now I knew that Isabel was too old for her part, but I never dreamed that the director would give her my role with a new leading man, and it certainly never occurred to me that Ivonne and Frank would retire so soon, leaving Phillip and me the part of the mature couple. And I must confess, she sobbed, that it never crossed my mind that you would die and leave me alone with nobody to confide in, she said, looking at her wrinkles reflected on the shiny surface of the casket.

No way they're going to make you the leading man, said Beatrice, smearing cream all over her face, when the leading "lady" is a little girl, just twenty-five years old. She could be your daughter! Be reasonable, Phillip, after all we're still in the play and that's what counts, said Beatrice. (And don't think I haven't seen you ogling her, you dirty old man, was what she didn't say.)

It's the rehearsals for the new opening night, Phillip, they get on my nerves, said Beatrice. Having the show temporarily closed down is like putting life on hold. I'm constantly on edge. Besides, did you notice all the changes Isabel is making in my role? Who does she think she is? I mean, I suppose it's natural for her to change a few little things to fit the character to her own personality, but so many changes? As if what I did all those years wasn't good enough, she said as she darkened her gray hairs in the mirror. "Monotonous and boring, lacking imagination," that's what she told me. But, what's wrong with her? I don't understand this new generation, she sighed. (Besides, I'm afraid. She wants to change everything, make it different, and if the play flops, what will we do? We're too old for new roles, was what she chose not to say.)

Don't cry, please, Beatrice, don't cry, said Isabel, watching her hiccup uncontrollably. The re-opening was a complete success. I thought the theater walls were going to fall down with all the applause and the critics praised my innovations beyond my wildest expectations, she said. (That's why you're crying, isn't it, Beatrice? Because envy is eating you alive, was what she didn't say.)

GALATEA

I don't want to begin to imagine the dreams and fantasies, the fears, deliriums, and secret anguish locked up in that golden cage where the canary lived during the time she was with me. I wish I could forget everything, even her name—"harder than marble, colder than snow"—Galatea, a name I chose especially because of her immaculate, white plumage.

To tell the truth, I thought she was a male when I bought her, a mistake well justified by her broad chest, the way she always held her head high even in her final days, as if she were extremely proud or incredibly stubborn, and the blinding beauty of her feathers. I harbored the illusion of adorning my solitude, first imposed and then consciously assumed, with the passionate song of a solitary male, but after hearing for several days the monotonous "chireep-chireep" of my recent purchase, I accepted the idea of sharing my monologue with someone of my same sex and destiny. We quickly grew fond of each other. She mesmerized me with her stark whiteness and turned out to be a flirtatious and intelligent companion. She never rebelled against being in a cage and soon learned how to take seeds from my hand and even from between my lips, as if giving me tiny kisses. She saved me from the indignity of talking to myself, as she responded to my voice with multiple "chireeps," obviously trying to communicate. Every morning her cheerful call awoke me. Inevitably I began to reveal to her my most intimate thoughts, my memories nourished by resentment and a thousand well-honed reasons for my celibacy, polished with a secret bitterness.

How many months went by? August, September, October, November. . .It wasn't until the end of January, with a breath of Spring in the air, that Galatea began to display marked variations in her usual hop-chireep-hop-chireep. She showed signs of a sudden increase in appetite, especially for fresh lettuce and cuttlebone, and she began to alternate her time on the perches with long scratch-and-peck sessions in the gravel at the bottom of the cage. By mid-February she had completely forgotten about her toy swing; she had abandoned the upper part of the cage and devoted herself body and soul to shredding the paper lining on the floor and plucking soft, fuzzy feathers from her chest in an obvious display of nesting instinct.

After some heavy soul searching and painful analysis, I realized the injustice of imposing my celibacy on Galatea, so I set out to find her a mate. I remember a passing illusion of family. I found a snow-white crested male with a clear, passionate song, who seemed as if he could satisfy all of Galatea's needs. I fell in love in her name, imagining how she would be irresistibly seduced by his virile attributes. I installed a small, gilded box for the nest and placed the male inside the virginal cage, but not without certain palpitations and a strange, tingling excitement. Then I sat down at a prudent distance to watch the courtship.

Galatea was duly modest. She glanced at the male with guarded reservation and continued to shred paper. The suitor fluttered around the cage ostentatiously, ruffled his feathers with blatant masculine vanity, tilted his head flirtatiously, and let out a heartfelt warble that Galatea ignored completely. Evidently my presence was bothersome so I retreated to the kitchen, imagining passionate copulation and silky sensations of fertility. I decided I wouldn't go back to the living room until the next morning. That night, in dreams, my fantasies mingled with the imagined yearnings of the canary.

The next day Galatea's cheerful chireep-hop-chireep woke me, and I hurried to the living room with the anxious expectation of a grandmother-to-be. The canary was hopping blithely from one perch to the other, calling to me as usual. For a moment I didn't see the male, and then I discovered him, huddled under the feeder, trembling and tattered. Many of his snow-white feathers were strewn around the bottom of the cage. Not knowing what to think, I sat down to observe. After a while the suitor, compelled by his undeniable instinct, came out of his hiding place, made a lopsided leap up to the perch and sidled over to Galatea before she could move. The female's eye squinted menacingly and with her beak she bashed her pursuer on the head with sudden and inexplicable ferocity. Then, in a flash, she grabbed the surprised suitor with beak and claws, and proceeded to beat him with her wings until the air was filled with blood and feathers. I rushed to the cage.

"Galatea!"

The canary released her prey at once and looked at me quizzically, almost with a smile, "Chireep?"

Horrified, I picked up the small, bloodied body, cradling it for a long time in the palm of my hand. It was still alive. During the twenty-four hours that I struggled in vain to save the canary's life I didn't once respond to Galatea's increasingly desperate chireeps. Finally I approached her cage and with an accusatory gesture, opened my hand wide, presenting her with the mangled corpse. Paralyzed on her perch, she gazed at the bundle of bloody feathers and then, suddenly, began to sing an eerie song that lasted until three in the afternoon. It was the last sound she ever made. The next morning I found the first egg: white, immaculate, and completely lifeless, a barren ovulation dropped on the floor of the cage. It made me sad to see it and I quickly threw it in the garbage. The next day the second egg appeared, identical to the first. The translucent emptiness of the little white shell exacerbated my anxiety and I threw it away immediately, without ceremony.

Thus began Galatea's irremeable descent into dementia. During the day she wore herself out in a flurry of nest making, tearing up paper and plucking out her feathers frantically. At night she was possessed by such a dark, uterine frenzy that in less than a month she delivered up the iniquitous sum of fifty-three empty eggs, all perfect in their virginal whiteness. My anxiety became impotence, insomnia, fear, hatred. I felt defenseless before the cruel and vacuous production, but all my efforts to stop it were in vain. During the entire crazed egg-laying process, Galatea never deceived herself. She never once tried to hatch the violent spoils. She just lay them, night after night, in a deranged ritual of ovarian expiation, while I suffocated under nightmares of infertile ovulations and death wishes.

Obviously that perverse ovipositing could not continue indefinitely. The slow, seedless suicide had to have an end. One morning I found Galatea stiff, on her side on the bottom of the cage, her minute, anguished existence snuffed out by the last, disproportionate egg that couldn't come out. I picked her up and squeezed her little body between my fingers: The egg emerged. It was a strange, copper color with an irregular shell, totally opaque. It felt heavy, as if it harbored something inside.

I tossed Galatea into the garbage can with no remorse or

tears, but for some reason I couldn't relinquish the egg. Every time I tried to throw it away, I was paralyzed by both anxiety and morbid fascination and would end up putting it back on that enormous white cushion where every day I incubate it a while with the feverish hope that some day it will hatch and reveal to me its fearful secret.

ADELAIDE'S BODY

No, it's not the solution
to throw yourself under a train like Tolstoy's Anna
or drink Madame Bovary's poison
or wait on the plain of Avila for the visit
by the angel with an arrow
until throwing a shawl on your head
and beginning to act.

Or surmise geometric laws by counting
beams on the ceiling of your cell
as Sor Juana did. It's not the solution
to write, while waiting for visitors,
in the living room of the Austen family
or shut yourself up in the attic
of some New England residence
and dream, with the Dickinson's Bible
under your old maid's pillow.

There must be another way that isn't called Sappho
or Messalina or Mary of Egypt
or Magdalene or Clemencia Isaura.

Another way of being human and free

Another way of being.

—Rosario Castellanos

The day the carpetlayer arrived, Adelaide met her Destiny. He was short, skinny, disheveled, and very macho. He had red hair and a beard. As he wove a net of smooth, beguiling words around Adelaide's beauty, he laid the carpet, and then he laid Adelaide herself on the carpet. He took her there the first time with the smell of new carpet tufts exciting her nose; then on her grandmother's sofa that exhaled ancestral dust with every thrust; twice under the dining room table while she saw Christmas lights and gave thanks and, in a final superhuman effort, he besieged her in the broom closet where he fell exhausted on the mouse droppings.

Adelaide straightened what was left of her skirt, while the redhead gathered his tools, snapped shut his toolbox and his fly, bade farewell with an arrogant gesture, and disappeared through the back door where he had entered just an hour earlier.

She never saw the carpetlayer again, nor did she ever have another carpet laid, or tidy any sofa, or mess up another skirt. She abandoned her house to dust and time and with iron determination began to pursue that Fatal Star that had shone for her under the table as the carpetlayer enjoyed something she couldn't understand. It didn't have anything to do with nocturnes by Chopin or exercises on the piano or cross-stitch embroidery or art history classes or the elaborate preparation of succulent meals for a future husband or knitting little sweaters for mothers-to-be or bridge parties on leisurely afternoons or rosaries for the dead or even that pleasurable and undoubtedly sinful sensation of washing certain parts of her body under the tepid caress of water. In other words it had nothing to do with anything that she had ever known.

Unknown or not, Adelaide was convinced that that was her Calling in Life and with her usual tenacity she dedicated herself to pursuing her new goal. Exactly how many bookstores she explored in search of ancient guides for her exercises or how many hours she spent prostrated before the makeshift altar with her forehead against the hard tile floor or how many days of fasting and sacrifice she endured or how many different names she invoked before hitting upon the one that corresponded to her century, will never be known because they are secrets that remained behind the closed door of her bedroom. But exactly at 11:59 P.M. on the second Saturday of May, just before the merciless hand of the clock marked the first hour of the date that is so stressful for the Wicked One, Mephistopheles grew tired of hearing such a string of nonsense and anachronisms in the sharp, persistent voice that silenced even the hissing of the infernal fires and decided to make an appearance in order to find out what the devil she wanted.

Satan arrived precisely at midnight. Adelaide was waiting for him in her blackest, tightest, most sensual dress. When she saw him she uttered the well-known but archaic formula of three, and awoke in the spirit of the Spirit a nostalgia for the ancient rhetoric.

"Oh, mysterious and morbid lady who so fearlessly and insistently invokes the Spirit of Evil, the Prince of Darkness, the Invincible Satan, the Fallen Angel, Lucifer, the Supreme Instigator of Sin! What dark, secret and impeccable. . .I mean, peccable purpose has moved you to such conjuration?"

Adelaide rejoiced upon hearing the tenebrous tones and stood upright and proud to deliver her plea.

"Oh, Indisputable King of the Dark Gloom, Sinister Prince, Ill-fated and Ill-favored, Malign Being invoked by me since I realized my malevolent and lascivious desire, night after night in the long nights of this winter of my life. . ."

"Get to the point, wench! Many barren women are waiting for me tonight so they can wake up mothers-to-be. I suppose you want the same."

". . .in the long nights of this winter of my life, who on this Transcendent Night, Unique and Inimitable, has deigned to respond to my black-hearted and unyielding faith by appearing. . ."

"Hush or I'll make you a zealot!"

". . .appearing in Perverse Person and in all your Turbulent Grandeur to grant me my only burning and ill-conceived desire, without which I would prefer to descend to the eternal fire rather than continue in this miserable world, I beg of you. . ."

". . .to make you a **mother**!" concluded Satan with a sigh of relief.

". . .to make me a **man**!" concluded Adelaide, piercing him with an implacable look.

"Impossible!"

"Don't recant! I am ready to sign with blood, saliva, or any other bodily fluid to close the deal and surrender my Soul to you for all of eternity."

Mephistopheles gave her an incredulous look and burst out laughing with such violence that he extinguished the devotional candles and set the curtains aflutter.

"You poor little, insignificant thing! Innocent and naive creature! Women don't have souls."

"But I thought. . ."

"Just spiritual demagoguery to keep you under control. I'm sorry. No merchandise, no deal. Arrivederci!"

Mephistopheles spun around on one foot and headed resolutely toward the door. Adelaide felt her last opportunity slipping away and she held out a trembling hand.

"Wait! If I have no soul, I will give you my body."

The Prince of Darkness stopped and turned slowly around, his astute glance caught by Adelaide's determined look.

"What good is it to me?" he asked cautiously.

"It's young, strong and healthy. It's got years of use ahead."

"It's imperfect, unstable, unpredictable, and in general, extremely defective."

"By no means," refuted Adelaide, slipping off her stockings and unbuttoning her blouse. "It's a perfect, natural clock; tireless, accommodating, and docile. It has an endless capacity for enduring pain and tedium; it harbors an ancestral resignation; it withstands humiliation and mistreatment. It is a source of temptation, an indecipherable enigma, deception of innocent souls, bitter sweetness, a lair of contradictions capable of confounding the wisest sage or the holiest saint; it requires very little upkeep and will never aspire to fame or glory. . ."

Adelaide let her voice fall along with her bra, as she approached her bidder and allowed him to inspect the merchandise: the firm breasts, the smooth thighs, the flexible back, the aroma of the neck, the softness of the belly, and the incessant undulation of the hips. The deal was closed with no further haggling.

"Tomorrow you will wake up a man, and your name will be Adel," Mephistopheles exclaimed, as he disappeared.

". . .and my trade: carpetlayer," sighed Adelaide before she fell asleep.

The day he arrived at Aida's house to lay the carpet, Adel met his Destiny. He was tall, handsome, blond, and seductive. As he wove a tapestry of sweet and insidious words around the beautiful body reclining on the sofa, he laid the honey-colored carpet and then he tried to lay Aida on the carpet, but she made him chase her all through the living room, around the table, across the sofa, into the kitchen, upstairs to the bedroom, and back downstairs until he managed to corner her in the broom closet and fall exhausted at her feet.

From that moment on, Adel was convinced that that was

his Calling in Life. He devoted himself night and day to the task of laying carpets so he could save enough money to dress that irresistible body with silk, adorn that smooth neck with pearls and diamonds, and bestow golden slippers on those tantalizing feet. He grew grey hairs and his skin became wrinkled as he labored endlessly, imagining in his solitude the ultimate possession of the body he so desired. In delirious dreams he constructed feverish altars for her and he saw her naked and tender, docile and resigned, fertile and submissive. Between carpet laying jobs he would visit her, giving her lavish gifts, kissing her feet, and besieging her with declarations of eternal, boundless love. Finally he reached his goal. On the afternoon of Holy Friday, Adel arrived at Aida's house dressed in a suit of pure silk. He was only ten years older but it looked like twenty; he had the latest-model automobile with a chauffeur, an enormous diamond ring, and a bank account with seven figures. He laid it all at her feet and asked her to marry him. When he heard her resounding "No!" he exclaimed with desperation, "But, woman! Have you no soul?"

Aida gave him an incredulous look and let forth a peal of delighted laughter that ruffled the curtains and made the crystal chandelier tinkle.

A BRIEF EXERCISE IN THE ABSURD

For twenty years we had been weaving the threads of time into a comfortable conjugal relationship, when he became distracted. At first I thought it a passing interest, an ephemeral attraction as we trudged up the slope of our forties. I cultivated a healthy patience, trying to ignore his dalliance, and invented convincing reasons to justify this sudden digression. So many years of living together. It was natural for him to maunder, to allow his drowsy instincts to awaken and his eye to wander in search of new horizons. The novelty. My rival galvanized his settledness, exhilarated his imagination with youthful yearnings and fantasies. The promises of adventure bedazzled him. I rehearsed tolerant smiles toward his engrossment and waited for the return of our tranquil evenings when we would synthesize our daily activities in a few words and share a peaceful monotony without interference.

I wasn't worried. Our relationship was irrevocable, though no longer ablaze. Comfortably lukewarm. A tapestry of common goals tightly woven with shared memories, whose specific and commanding presence assured us of continuity over and above any desire to wipe a clean slate. I just had to give him time. I decided to wait without changing our routine, feigning indifference. I pretended not to notice when, spurred on by my competitor, he had hair transplants to cover his bald spot, abandoned his conservative suits in favor of a youthful indulgence in denim, bathed himself with Brut, and bought a machine with an electric band that shook the spare tires around his bourgeois belly. I told myself five hundred times a day that my adversary wasn't taking anything from me; after all, our sex life had been substituted long ago for an insipid tenderness that slowly had degenerated into sleepy complacency. Cuddled up next to him in bed, I closed my eyes, knowing that his warmth and his presence were mine even if his imagination belonged to the provocative visions of my opponent.

When two months had passed and the problems remained unremedied, I ran crying to my mother. Resignation and patience, she said. Don't try to get between them, and don't play the victim. Two things bedevil a man: guilt and prohibition. The first drives him to obsession and the second makes him dig in his heels. Feign ignorance, give him some rope. A loose bronco soon tires of bucking. Meekly I returned home, caressing a nascent humiliation. I blanketed his blatant indifference with kisses and wrapped myself tightly in my own impotence. His lethargic apathy outlined my stubborn routine and our habits, because of his distraction, resounded in emptiness.

When six months had passed, I was wallowing in profound solitude, plagued by neglect and inertia, so lacking in caresses and attention that, by default, the stillness echoed inside me. I wandered through the empty shell of our marriage, dragging my dejection behind, while my enemy entertained him with myriad visions of exotic possibilities. His progressive alienation was punctuated by increasingly prolonged evasions and even my quiet presence seemed to make him bristle. With my silence I offered an opaque resistance to his meager attempts at denial. Slowly, my well-worn patience began crumbling and my quiet resignation crackled with spates of rebellion. To hell with my mother's advice! I decided to take the fort.

It was our anniversary. I beguiled my usual humanities with a brisk bath and sheathed them in libidinous black lace and satin. An anointment of fragrant creams unleashed the subdued lasciviousness of my flesh and my body prepared to entoil that other body whose indifference emulated scorn. With nearly obscene violence I unleashed my hair from the accustomed bun and let it drape, lush and wanton, over my bare shoulders. Champagne on ice, two candles flickering light and shadow across an intimate table and a lusty, come-hither perfume. I lay down on the sofa, carefully accentuating the sinuous curve of my hips and waited, rehearsing the onset of a suggestive tremor.

When he arrived I lowered my eyes so as not to unclothe his naked surprise. The nostalgic tones of a violin scarcely ruffled the stillness. Slowly, I dared look at him looking at me. He arched his eyebrows. I interpreted excitement. He turned and went up the stairs. The wait was electrifying. I imagined his just-bathed torso, sprouting curly chest hairs, framed by the silk lapels of his oriental robe. I strained my ears to hear the footsteps that would signal an end to the inexorable crawling of time. Nothing. The silence throttled my humiliated throat and a debilitating cramp decimated my body's crystalline illusion. He wasn't going to come down!

Frenzied, I attacked the steps two by two. He was stretched out on the bed, cuddled in grungy pajamas and, judging by the obsessive glaze over his eyes, engrossed in thoughts and images that had nothing to do with my pleasure. I exploded in wails of despair and reproach, bitterly lacrimating my solitude and sadness. One by one I hurled at him his vows and promises, shredding our fantasy a duo, with a holy brouhaha that would end all pretense forever. Finally, I ushered him my irrevocable ultimatum:

"You can't have us both! It's either me or that, that, that. . ." I stammered, gesturing wildly.

"Amalia, for God's sake! Let's not behave like children. We've had a lot of good years. Let's not lose respect for each other now." And he went back to entertaining his faraway fantasies.

That's why I'm packing my tear-sodden clothes, stuffing into the corners of the suitcase knotted-up memories of twenty years and thinking that maybe, just maybe, it would have been better to follow my mother's advice for a little while longer and wait patiently for him to tire of the damned television.

TRILOGY

1. Lillith

The Non-beginning

God created the earth, but the earth had no support so beneath the earth He created an angel. But the angel had no support so beneath the angel's feet He created a large rock made of ruby. But the rock had no support so beneath the rock He created a bull with four thousand eyes, ears, noses, mouths, tongues and feet. But the bull had no support so beneath the bull He created a fish called Bahamut, and beneath the fish he put water, and below the water he put darkness, and human science sees no further than that.

—Arab tradition, Jorge Luis Borges

In the beginning God created the earth and the skies. The earth was confusing and empty, and darkness covered the face of the abyss, and God, who was young and ingenuous, marveled at all He had created. Like a great child illuminated by goodness and innocence, He pointed here and there making the stars appear and then the black holes, the animals and minerals, matter and antimatter, fish, birds, plants, and everything else.

In spite of his omnipotence and divine wisdom, God did not have much experience creating universes so it was natural for him to make a few mistakes. For example, at the beginning of the sixth day He said, "Let's make Man in our image and likeness, so he can reign over the fish in the sea and the beasts of the earth," and He created human beings in his image and He created them male and female united back to back so they would be equal and of the same material. He named the male Adam and the female Lillith.

During the first one hundred utopian years, Adam and Lillith proved to be fundamentally incompatible: The dorsal bond, although it kept them together and at the same time pure, also kept them from knowing and loving each other like the rest of the species.

God pondered this dilemma for three centuries while Adam and Lillith, each one developing individually as well as mutually, suffered the clashes of will experienced by any Siamese twins and ended up lurching about on the sweet grasses of Eden, kicking, scratching, and punching each other as best they could.

The usually peaceful Garden of Eden was filled with such cries and insults that God took less than the prescribed 150,000 years to effect a mutation. He lifted his flaming Sword of Justice, raised his voice to impose infinite stillness on the Garden and its inhabitants, and with almost omniscient precision, he sundered the bodies that had been united. It would have been a perfect maneuver, except for a slight tremor at the last moment that made his divine sword swerve millimetrically, leaving Lillith with a bit more buttocks than Adam. But the mistake was so minute that God chose to ignore it and declared his work well done. With a magnanimous gesture He dissolved the ban on movement; the Universe resumed functioning in a more or less orderly fashion, and God, creating in a flash the law of inertia, prepared himself to enjoy a well-deserved rest.

Meanwhile back in Eden, Adam and Lillith were waking up from the profound hush that occurs when the cosmos stands still and for the first time gazing at each other face to face. Oh, divine discovery! Oh, supreme miracle! Equal and, nevertheless, different. The last interrupted insult died in Lillith's mouth and during the long silence of amazed contemplation, the joyous sounds of Eden could be heard once more: the birds' singing, the river's gurgling, the breeze weaving poetry with the leaves of the trees. And oh, miracle of miracles: the human sigh. It was love at first sight, each with the other and then with themselves and their own bodies. Comparative analysis gave rise to individual pride. Adam quickly constructed an altar to his phallus while Lillith did the same in honor of her womb; then, with the independence of separate bodies, they each worshipped first at their own altar and then at the other's.

They exercised their freedom by running in opposite directions until meeting at the other end of the Garden, thus uniting the extremes. There they closed their eyes as if floating in one of God's dreams, and wandered with their hands over each other's flesh, searching with their touch for what their eyes could not perceive. They discovered pleasure and tickling, caresses and pinches; Adam recognized his piece of buttock cleaved to Lillith's gluteal area and was overwhelmed with tenderness for the part ceded to the other's body. Their fights turned into laughter; their insults, into sighs. Peace returned to the Garden, at least for as long as they were unaware of the specific functions of their notable differences, and God continued dreaming about the creation of future universes, each one more perfect than the previous.

But ever since the non-beginning of all time, the mating

season was destined to arrive, and the order that God himself had given to go forth and multiply came into force, not for the sublime purpose of animal pleasure, but simply to delegate to others the monotonous task of mass production.

One morning at the beginning of the ninth century after Creation and long before God had planned to wake up from his nap, a great disturbance shook the Garden at its very roots, waking the Primordial Pair from their Edenic sleep. The ecstatic trembling of trees and flowers, of ivy and grass, unleashed into the air such a quantity of pollen that bees went crazy and appointed more queens than they could fertilize; dragonflies executed fantastic copulatory dances in the air until they collapsed on the ground to lay their eggs; and fish performed astounding aquatic acrobatics as they scattered eggs and sperm throughout the waters. The animals of the fields, the jungles, the mountains, and the plains chased and mounted each other with such jubilation and such paradisiacal bellowing that they shook the four corners of the Garden. Birds flew in allegorical pirouettes until their wings gave out and they landed in the trees, obsessed with nesting. This multitude of caterwauls, sighs, chirps, and grunts tantalized the innocent ears of Adam and Lillith; their naive nostrils were titillated by the smell of œstrus and semen; and the image of copulation repeated a thousand times before their eyes set off in their pure and virginal minds the spark of procreative frenzy.

For the first time Adam's magnificent phallus arose like an omnipotent totem; for the first time Lillith's soft, round womb secreted its warm, maddening juices. With a proud cry, Lillith started a jubilant race around the Garden with Adam in hot pursuit. For five delirious days, with delight and laughter, silent pleasure and shouts of euphoria, he chased her. Finally, on the afternoon of the fifth day, with all the preliminary possibilities explored and the opponents exhausted, Adam and Lillith found themselves exactly in the middle of the Garden, panting and proud, exhibiting their magnificent plumage. Suddenly, Adam pointed peremptorily to the ground:

"Get down, woman, I'm going to mount you!"

"The hell you are!" replied Lillith indignantly. "We're face to face now and who knows, we might get stuck together again."

"Well then, lie on your back and I'll cover you like a real man."

"You lie on *your* back. Why should I be the one on the ground?"

"Because the stake goes into the ground. . .and **I** have the **stake**!"

"Don't yell at me!"

Thus Edenic peace was shattered once more by Adam's and Lillith's shouts and insults that made even the smallest animals' fuzzy cheeks blush. All the other inhabitants of the Garden paused in their coupling to watch the war between the humans, and throughout the realm of Eden there arose such a clamor that God awoke from his divine siesta and hurried to see what was happening. When He saw Adam desperately badgering Lillith with his male organ and Lillith refusing with her legs firmly crossed, He knew that He had made a serious mistake.

God raised his hand once more and stopped the Universe, leaving the opponents suspended in mid-battle for more than a millennium while He rapidly reviewed the potential consequences of his error. The thunder of interminable marital combats roared in his ears, leading undoubtedly to Divine Insomnia and Justified Rage, and He quickly arrived at the conclusion that only complete annihilation would end the imperfection of the Universe, and He would have to start all over again on some other day of Eternity. And, feeling his

Spirit heavy with the great sadness caused by his Most Perfect Decision, He re-initiated the movement of the Cosmos in order to announce the End to his creatures.

But, in the instant in which Lillith regained mobility, she faced her Creator and, filled with rage and resentment, pronounced the Ineffable Name. She was immediately endowed with wings and transported out of Eden to an unknown region of the cosmos beyond Divine Jurisdiction. The Just Finger stopped in mid-air and the Most Perfect Decision was forever silenced. Frustrated in his desire to impose justice on Lillith who was now immortal, God had to resort to a partial remedy. With a profound sigh He immersed Adam in a deep slumber, took one of his ribs, closed the gap with flesh, and formed a woman from Adam's rib. He presented her to Adam, who exclaimed:

"This creature is surely flesh of my flesh and blood of my blood!"

And God went back to a somnolence which grew more and more uneasy as time went by.

The Region Of Fallen Angels And Other Divine Debris

In the insomniac space that separates
fruit from flower, thought
from the action that engenders isolation,
death by needles awaits me.

—José Gorostiza

Transported out of Eden and catapulted to an unknown cosmic region, enveloped in a sticky brume much like grey cotton candy, stripped of the clarity and mental splendor of innocence by her unprecedented act, Lillith experienced for the first time the burden of solitude, the anguish of doubt, the infinite expanse of ignorance, and the chaos of comprehension. Overwhelmed by nostalgia, her only thought was to return to Eden without delay.

The abrupt transition had erased from her memory the recent problems with Adam, leaving only the sensation of an enormous void that was slowly being filled with the cloudiness of reason. She hastened her flight. In the distance she could see the luminous dome that separated the Garden from the turbid accumulation of knowledge floating in the outer regions of space, and she sped toward it. However, upon approaching, the brilliance of primal innocence pierced her consciousness like a vengeful sword and she began to fall helplessly.

During that long, slow fall within the enormous circumference of the universe, Lillith for the first time began to question the reason for existence, to blur the distinction between fantasy and reality, and to confuse in the nocturnal confines of her memory the perfect delimitation between truth and falsehood. During the descent she lost all notion of up or down, and immediately understood the triviality of positions and directions. Suddenly an image of Adam, with his finger pointing firmly toward the ground, flooded her memory, and she fainted.

When she awoke she was on the shore of the Red Sea. Behind her stretched a desolate landscape, a forbidding plain, interrupted here and there by gigantic dunes of gray sand and, farther in the distance, by some abrupt, black buttes that mercilessly cleaved the sand. The hot, humid air tasted of salt and seemed to flow in and out of her without leaving a trace. Vapors escaped continuously from the body of languid water, and as they rose they congealed in the ashen sky; a murky pallor filtered through the mist, blurring the already indefinite outline of things. A long, reddish tongue of water licked the surface of its shores and irregular puffs of air stirred the dusty sand, tinting parts of the sky with ocher. With the lucidity of her new consciousness, Lillith understood that she had lost forever the possibility of returning to Eden.

In spite of its appearance, the Red Sea was not uninhabited. It was populated by castaways from the first unskilled attempts at Divine Creation: fallen angels, aquatic demons, basilisks and serpents with two heads, mono-winged birds that flew in interminable circles around the rocky buttes, and ridiculous five-footed cats that stumbled around aimlessly. Lillith met them all on her first night there. The fallen angels and winged demons accepted her immediately as one of them, trying to alleviate her nostalgia with perverse games and copulations in unimaginable positions.

Lillith threw herself into the merriment with all the fervor of vengeance and soon forgot Adam. Finding her procreative faculties overdeveloped, she began to give birth to a hundred demons a day, which she spewed across the Red Sea as fish spread sperm in the river. To save time she called them all *Lillin* and, pursuing her amorous diversions, abandoned them to their fate.

She soon discovered the absurd monotony of reproduction, the tedium of unbridled sex, the mortal boredom of immortality, the meaninglessness of existence, the solitude of companionship, the vacuity of love, the futility of knowledge, the ambiguity of truth, the usefulness of lies, and the indifference of God. These discoveries immersed her in a profound melancholy that lasted until the day she met the hyena. An absurd combination of wild animal and clown, this creature represented one of the All Powerful's attempts at originality, but had to be expelled from Eden for irreverence before the

Perfect Solemnity. The hyena cured Lillith of her malaise, providing her with antidotes to life: bitter laughter, mocking cynicism, black humor, and the exaltation of the absurd. When she finally managed to comprehend the omniscient joke, she let forth a peal of laughter that traversed the nebulous curtain and pitilessly terminated the Divine Siesta.

The Fall

Then, only then, when we are both alone,
we know that not love but dark death
makes us contemplate each other face to face,
eye to eye,
to join together and embrace, more than
alone and adrift,
even more, and still more and more.

—Xavier Villaurrutia

The day of the densest fog, or rather, the afternoon of the heat that enveloped everything like an amorphous mass of damp clay, just when liquid air was merging with the vaporous water and precisely five minutes before Lillith gave up trying to dry her wings, the magpie arrived.

The magpie is the nineteenth mistakenly-endowed creation of the first and only epoch of Eden. She suffers from incurable verbal diarrhea: Everything that enters her eyes or ears goes immediately out through her beak, due to a misplaced orifice. Since in the beginning Truth was One and Indivisible, the magpie was not a problem, and God allowed her to roam freely around the Garden pestering every creature with ears.

However, after the unfortunate events with Adam, Lillith, and the Ineffable Name, God omni-intuited the danger that the knowledge of Error represented for his Paradise, and instituted the Judicious Censorship, commanding that every Truth carry the seal of his Divine Authorization before it could be publicly distributed. Since all else should be considered vile lies, he endowed his creatures with the capacity to deny what they saw and discredit what they heard, unless it was divinely authorized. He erased from Adam's memory the image of Lillith and all recollection of the delightful hours spent with her, leaving only a confused yearning engraved in a dark corner of his subconscious. In Eve He implanted the firm conviction that she was the First Woman, and He imposed complicity on the animals by making their language incomprehensible to humans.

Nevertheless, the magpie didn't attend the Divine Council in which these adjustments to Reality took place. Always eager to find someone who would listen to her, she was on the far side of the Garden initiating a new pair of ears that belonged to the serpent called Sammaël. Therefore, she wasn't informed of the uprooting of the Ancient Truth and the implantation of the New, nor was she affected by the prohibition on communication between humans and animals.

Upon returning to the center of the Garden, she came upon Eve and, lighting on her shoulder, poured into the First Woman's tender ears the whole story of the Other. If Eve did not react like Lillith, pronouncing the Ineffable Name and being transported out of Eden, it was only due to her origin as a rib. She cried silently for thirty days and thirty nights, forever opening up her tear ducts, forging in her soul the invincible vocation of martyrdom, acquiring a maddening capacity for self-sacrifice, and cultivating a secret and twisted desire for vengeance. When she finally dried her tears and repaired the damage done to her eyes, Eve had the bitter secret buried in the depths of her heart.

Faced with the impossibility of directly attacking the flesh of which she was flesh, she became more servile and docile than ever, attending to all of Adam's needs—both real and imagined—to such an extent that he was left with nothing to do but lean comfortably against the Tree of Life and sleep.

Absolute idleness produced an urgency in the First Man's subconscious with its constant demand for dream material, and it was necessary to resurrect his blurry memories of Lillith. Thus there began to appear on his oneiric screen the figure of a woman with long hair and fiery eyes, whose playful cavorting and exciting caresses made him wake up trembling with desire and eagerly calling for Eve. Unfortunately, Eve was always busy in the endless, time-consuming tasks that she had invented for herself, and at nightfall she gave an exhausted sigh and fell asleep immediately, leaving Adam to frustrated thoughts of imminent violations.

That was the status quo when the magpie took it upon herself to inform Eve of the serpent's existence, praising his virtues of tolerance and understanding; Eve couldn't resist the temptation to meet him. Sammaël was waiting for her, coiled up in a tree, an ancestor of the willow that later would be called the Tree of Good and Evil, but that at the time had no name. Eve sat down beneath the tree and was surprised to see her image reflected in Sammaël's unfathomable little eyes as he contemplated her. That day the serpent provided Eve with the consolation of confession and the relief of uncontrolled sobbing and infused her with the imperious need for mitigation. Her visits became a habit. Day after day Eve lay in the shade of the willow tree and poured into the immutable ears of the serpent all her frustration and sadness born of love's first disenchantment. Sammaël listened to her with endless patience as he slid the tip of his tail along her trembling thighs and rested his head between her voluptuous breasts.

The Corrected and Authorized Version of Events in Eden that reached Adam's ears said something about an apple and since he had eaten apples the previous day, he supposed that those were the fruit in question. Eve corroborated that version.

The fact is that when God finally decided to wake up from his long nap and pulled his head out from under the cloud that had protected him from the hilarious laughter of Lillith and the hyena, He saw something that exhausted his Divine Patience and, pointing with a trembling, white finger toward the Pearly Gates of Paradise, He expelled Adam, Eve, and the magpie forever.

The magpie was off in a flash, searching for someone who would listen to the story, and she found Lillith sitting on the banks of the Red Sea, drying her wings. Lillith, listening carefully to the news that would offset the weight of cynicism in her soul with the levity of hope, recalled the delicious days of Eden, the crazed fleeing and pursuing of the mating season, and Adam's first sigh that had lodged in her heart. She felt an unaccustomed flutter of butterflies in her stomach which she confused with love and, thanking the magpie, set off in search of Adam.

Paradises Lost

Fleeing. . .fleeing. . .fleeing. . .
I am fleeing the Wind and the Sea.

I want to escape the howl
and the sob. . .

Return to the cloud. . .
There is a still cloud up there, that waits for me

—León Felipe

While it is difficult, sometimes impossible, to forget your First Love, it is even more impossible to recover it. Distances and differences beyond the dominion of reason intervene and inexorably surround the soft tissues of the heart.

Separating the outskirts of Eden, where Adam finally arrived at a lasting truce with Eve and for the first time sank his shovel into the ground and his flesh into his flesh, from the shores of the Red Sea, there was much more than distance, much more than social differences or conflicting customs, more than clothing that isolated the sexes: There was the unbridgeable expanse between mortality and immortality.

Lillith, expelled from Paradise by her own volition, was ignorant of the shame of guilt, the fear of freedom, the dread of death, the hope of salvation, and, especially, the force of habit that Eve had imposed on her partner. Adam, on the other hand, diligently informed about the State of Things by the Maximum Authority, could not comprehend childbirth without pain, intercourse without hierarchy, integration of opposites, absence of limits, and acceptance of absurdity, although he did manage to recognize immediately his piece of ass on Lillith's fanny.

In spite of these obstacles, their relationship lasted almost 130 years, since neither could renounce the longing for the absolute or accept the reality of frustration. For Adam it was a race against time with the hope of recuperating immortality through love, if only for a moment, as well as the beginning of an irreversible triangular pattern in his emotional configuration. Lillith, in turn, feeling the desperation of immortality, sought in each embrace the secret of death and the mysterious vibrations of finite lives.

They surrendered to their passion with an earnestness and anxiety that left them exhausted and trembling, but it was all in vain: Nothing—not their fervid embrace, not Lillith's pride, not Adam's stubbornness—could recapture that first moment of glorious communion they experienced during the mating season in Eden. Their union was destined to fail, something Eve knew from the beginning, so she waited with patience and resignation, confident in the strength of her weapons. And she was right. While fulfilling his conjugal duties, Adam gave Eve the pretext she needed to demand his return home: He begat Seth.

On the second day of October in the 129th year after the Expulsion from Eden, Adam renounced his search for immortality. Eve received his homecoming without recrimination, closing the door behind him. According to the Authorized Version, they had many children and Adam lived 800 more years. Information about Lillith, however, is scarce, since she has been relegated to the region of forbidden myths. The details of her existence are material for stories that grandmothers like to tell at nightfall to scare mischievous little girls. Nonetheless, we can suppose that the humiliation of being abandoned for Eve has left deep scars in her soul. It is rumored that all this time she has been plotting her revenge, seducing mortals in their sleep to produce human descendants who sooner or later will overthrow the daughters of Eve and occupy their place, but there is no proof of this.

11. Sammaël

The Search

Guard: You're here now.
Man: They brought me here while I was asleep. I didn't ask for anything. I didn't tell anyone to bring me here.
Guard: But you're here now.

—León Felipe

Sammaël wasn't a Divine Creation strictly speaking since he had sprung from the Omniscient Subconscious—by spontaneous generation—during one of God's frequently interrupted naps. What's more, Sammaël was not even a creation, but rather a materialization of all that had been rejected and repressed by the Immaculate Decency, which explains not only his beauty but also the Divine Desperation upon awakening and finding him entwined in the willow chatting with the mesmerized Eve. His immediate response to recognizing Sammaël's origin was total denial. God refused to believe that the subconscious could materialize its contents without Divine Consent and chose to completely ignore the bastard's existence. Therefore Sammaël wasn't informed of the Fall or the Expulsion, and, when peace and quiet descended upon Eden once again, the solitary occupant of the willow coiled up to wait for Eve's return.

But Eve did not appear then nor on the following days, and Sammaël's patience—as long and thin as his body—began to wane. During his wait he discovered a tangible meaning of eternity and began to fill it up first with the memory of Eve's eyes, mouth, breasts, thighs, voice and tears, sighs and trembling, and then with imaginary variations on the same themes until he exhausted the entire repertoire of his brief experience. Finally he understood that hope and despair go hand in hand, and the desire to be loved often results in prolonged frustration. And, riddled by the bite of sharp-toothed solitude from his head to the tip of his pointed tail, Sammaël slid down the tree trunk until he came to rest on the body-print that Eve had left in the memorable grass of Eden, and transformed himself.

Although the serpent has been blamed for the loss of Paradise, he should be commended for the discretion he showed by not performing this astonishing metamorphosis before the susceptible eyes of the First Woman, thus leaving her the option of returning to Adam. Tall, strong, lusty, with jet-black hair, a tan face, green eyes filled with seductive iridescence, and strange, pointed ears that often would be confused with horns, Sammaël was indeed enthralling. He had kept all his viperine harmony and grace, and the fluid sinuosity of each movement revealed his double nature. Thus, with amazing, languid sensuality, he separated his body from the nostalgic impression of the other body, and, rising up in the image of the one whose image he had found so many times in his Beloved's eyes, he set out in search of Eve with a truly moving optimism.

By then the frenetic reproductive activity of the First and Only Mating Season had degenerated into a monotonous nesting flurry, with mammals, reptiles, and birds scurrying and flitting around in search of hollow trees, burrows, lairs, or dens, all of which reminded Sammaël of Eve's domestic obsession. When he discovered at the base of the Tree of Life the meticulous, rigid, unnatural order of his Beloved, he wept green tears of yearning that left on his tongue, for the first time, the true salt of life.

In her frantic eagerness to clean, straighten, and accommodate, Eve had left behind on the polished surface of the Garden's ground, a wake of tidiness, a trail of unmistakable orderliness that stretched from the immaculately trimmed Tree, between the borders of red tulips, down the neat pathway of smooth pebbles, all the way to the plaza paved with precious stones, right in front of the Pearly Gates of Paradise. There Sammaël suddenly realized that he had been abandoned: Eve had not even bid farewell!

Overwhelmed by the bitterness of scorn, the rancid flavor of neglect, the sting of rejection, and the insipidness of indifference, Sammaël observed the barren, thirsty expanse of landscape that surrounded Eden and perceived beauty to be a concrete image of his own abandonment. And, finding the contemplation of it a partial relief from his loneliness, he sat down a while to look at God's work in all its equivocal splendor.

As he digested that sadness that could be called pristine, he discovered in the height of the mountains, the depth of the valleys, and in the branches of the trees, the secret of their roots. He recognized that the serpent invariably bites its tail, and understood that in the precarious equilibrium of the world his own existence was absolutely necessary for the continued existence of God—although the inverse was not necessarily true—and that the only unchangeable thing in Creation was the dust to which all would inevitably return. But for some strange reason, he didn't manage to formulate the idea of death that had been implanted so suddenly in the minds of Adam and his Wife, and this fundamental omission made him feel certain he could find Eve and stay with her for all eternity. Thus, carrying his vain illusion and with hope as an incentive, Sammaël slipped past the strict vigilance of the Cherub at the Gate and set off across the desert in search of his Beloved.

The Abyss

> *Alas! It is all an abyss—desire, action, dreaming, words!*
>
> —Baudelaire

Some say that he fell and others that he was flung, but in an unknown and forgotten Apocryphal Version it is affirmed, with a list of errata, that his descent was voluntary and possibly quite slow. Therefore, we can suppose that Sammaël, wandering through the desert in his futile search for Eve, discovered the mouth of the Abyss. He was overwhelmed by an unexpected yearning to Return and, confusing the Terrestrial Intestine with the Celestial Subconscious (a serpentine confusion of extremes), he embarked upon the equally futile search for his origins.

In the same Apocryphal Version we read the following: "It is not known for how long before the epoch of the Abyss, Sammaël wandered through the desert," (The Authorized Version denies, of course, that it was forty days and forty nights, but doesn't provide a trustworthy number either.) "opening the pores of his curiosity, perceiving the magnetism of the unknown, savoring the vitality of doubt and the enormity of imagination until he arrived at the edge of the depths. Nothing is known about his existence in the Abyss during all those millennia, but what can be affirmed without a doubt is that when he returned to the surface of the earth, Sammaël had deep, dark shadows under his beautiful green eyes."

Given such vast areas of ignorance, the few facts affirmed by the anonymous author have lost their power to convince, and, in recent years, a well-known group of scholars has questioned not only Sammaël's descent into the Abyss, but also the very existence of such a place. They have even mentioned the possibility that everything that has been said and continues to be said *ad nauseam* might be just a bunch of rumors, gossip, slander, conspiracy, tall tales, and lies propagated by Somebody in order to defame the one who properly speaking could be called "the first Son of God."

Nevertheless, in spite of the omissions in the Apocryphal Version, something is known about the epoch of the Abyss because it could be deciphered between the lines of the Authorized Version and passed from mouth to ear with the ensuing distortions. It seems that while officially they spoke of the deafening sound of grinding teeth and the roaring of infernal fire, down in that enormous planetary intestine full of festering bubbles there reigned a silence so opaque and concrete that for the first time Sammaël doubted his own existence and realized that language is the only proof of our luminous passage through the eternal dead of night, and even so it is not irrefutable. Actually, the so-called "Place of Lost Souls," "Prison for Rebel Angels," "Tormenters' Hideout," "Den of Demons and other Fallen Fools," was so solitary and abandoned that only the echo of his own thoughts alleviated Sammaël's deepening desperation. After so much thinking, he began to imagine that at an infinitely distant fixed point, parallel lines would meet and at that invisible and ineffable place lay the Origin of Things, including his own —which he so foolishly sought at the bottom of the Abyss—and also God's. Only then he understood that even if that were true, the interminable circle of Existence makes any Return eternally impossible, not because History varies by a thousandth of a millimeter, nor because the monotonous repetition of things and events is not identical with each cycle, or because one doesn't return to exactly the same place in exactly the same situation at exactly the same time, but simply since on the circular journey a person himself changes and then, worn down by the movement, polished by the peregrination, re-aligned by the voyage, and with the constant readjustment of the transmigration, identical things are seen with different eyes, which makes them unrecognizable always and forever. All that remains of memory is an occasional, vague sensation of déjà vu.

The effect of knowledge on the serpentine soul was crushing. For thousands of years he wandered like a madman through the earth's intestines, howling over his solitude and pouring out his justified rage against an injustice with no Name. The echoes of his lamentations and bitter complaints were infinitely multiplied in that deep void and perhaps that's why it's known as the "Wailing Grounds." It is possible that these sorrowful sounds reached the ears of Adam and Eve, and perhaps they traveled all the way to the smaller but more sensitive ears of Lillith, who was in a distant region of space at the far end of the cosmos, mourning her rootless condition and plotting her revenge. But the only thing we know for sure is that while Adam was fretting over his doubt about the paternity of Cain, and Eve was concocting logical explanations for their first son's green eyes, Sammaël curled himself into an unfamiliar fetal position that resembled his serpentine coils and began to carefully compare the insensitive and earthly Darkness of the Abyss with the insensitive and divine Darkness of the Subconscious and with the insensitive and unknown Darkness of the Womb in order to discern if in one of those three empty places he might find the reason and cause of his absolute, unbearable Orphanhood. The only thing he could distinguish was a slight trace of warmth in the imagined uterine darkness that reminded him of the first warmth perceived between Eve's breasts and he immediately capsized in a sea of infinite nostalgia. He relived the searing pain of separation, confronted the inevitable failure of each individual existence, and understood the overwhelming significance of a loss whose expression was as ineffable as the true name of God. That's probably when the circles under his eyes deepened. Given the undeniable truth of things, he understood that the only possible way to survive was by telling himself merciful lies and grasping at the straw of hope for reunion, so he wouldn't drown. At that moment he knew he was condemned to search for Eve and search again and again and again. . .

Earth, Smoke, Dust, Shadow, Nothing

Thine hands have made me and fashioned me
together round about; yet thou dost destroy me.
Remember, I beseech thee, that thou hast made
me as the clay; and wilt thou bring me into dust again?
Hast thou not poured me out as milk,
and curdled me like cheese?
. . .
And these things hast thou hid in thine heart?

Book of Job, 10: 8-13

Angry protest was not in Eve's nature, nor open rebellion in Adam's, rather they clung to submission and resentment. He did not shout and she did not curse; they practiced patience, resignation, and a passive resistance capable of undermining the stoicism of boulders. They received their Punishment without a sigh, and, actually, without comprehending. With compliance, and the indifference that ignorance lends, they surrendered to the new State of Things. Only Eve perceived a faint taste of earth on her tongue; it was so bitter that she spat on the ground. Adam, happy to have something to do at last, was so busy building the first house so Eve could exercise her newfound domestic vocation in a proper environment, that he didn't notice a slight flavor of primal matter in his mouth.

In fact, they were both quite content, enjoying the productivity of the earth and the reproductivity of Eve, until the unfortunate events with Cain, Abel, and the Divine Preference, undoubtedly caused by Omniscient Arbitrariness. Cain's exile and Abel's death, besides being a drastic loss of manpower immediately resented by Adam, opened doors to the dark understanding of the new Destiny of Mankind. When they saw the earth soak up the blood of their son and convert it to dust, Adam and Eve grasped the meaning of mortality and were overwhelmed by incommensurate sadness at their own finitude.

Eve produced a new torrent of tears, which she carefully gathered in a small bowl so as not to muddy her recently swept floor. That night, sitting on the edge of the rustic bed that Adam had built for her, with her face illuminated by the moonlight that shone through the window and her greying hair blown by a slight autumn breeze, she contemplated her reflection in the little lachrymatory. Incredulous, she ran her fingers along the outside of her eyes, feeling every wrinkle, every crack, every sign of corruption and decadence. The grooves around her mouth made that wellspring of words into an opaque sun with dark rays; the deep, wavy furrows in her forehead seemed to be no more than a graveyard for corn or wheat. The mesh of tiny wrinkles in her sunken cheeks and the dark, deflated bags under her eyes were empty wrappings of time already spent. With her bony hands she cradled her flaccid, dry breasts, once overflowing with nourishment for Cain, Abel, Seth, and even for Adam, who wanted to know what it felt like to have a mother. She felt the fragile skin of her belly, the hard, blue veins of her hands, the flap of hide under her arms, the folds of her double chin, her scrawny legs, and she noticed her withered look reflected in the shiny surface of tears. Faced with the reality of old age and the imminence of dust, she sought, with sudden and desperate ardor, the man who slept at her side, hoping to stir up the dust of both, and create a veritable Duststorm of offspring that would immortalize them for all time.

Adam was snoring, exhausted by the experience of having to dig a hole six feet deep, three feet wide and six feet long, and fill it up again immediately. Even though it seemed gratuitous to bury labor with labor or cover dust with dust, Adam felt compelled to ward off the vultures that threatened to hasten the transformation of matter with an intermediate step that the First Man didn't even want to imagine. When Eve woke him with her sudden, desperate passion, Adam was dreaming the dream of Sysiphus, eternally digging and filling in holes, and he lacked time to relate Eve's hotblooded advances to the blood that had flowed between the furrows of their field, so he didn't perceive the profound significance of her desire, nor did he agree to satisfy her. Instead, he defended his worn-out body the best he could and, tenderly but firmly rejected her offer.

"Eve, for God's sake!"

"No, Adam. For my sake!"

"But, let's wait for a better moment. It's the middle of the night and I'm beat; even my testicles ache."

The sting of being rejected is greater than the guilt of rejecting, so Eve overestimated her humiliation and converted it into irate indignation. When she saw that it was impossible to rouse Adam and his family jewels, she felt overwhelmed by her own impotence and howled with rage. When Adam began snoring again, she stomped her feet, pulled her hair out by the handful, ground her teeth, and tore at her clothes. Finally, she shouted at the top of her lungs, "You don't love me anymore!" and collapsed in a heap of uncontrollable sobs.

Eventually Adam managed to calm her down by rocking her as if she were a newborn baby, thus initiating the ritual of misunderstood gestures, crossed conversations, blaming, repeated accusations, general miscommunication, arguing and reconciliation that constitutes human "love."

From then forth the days assumed the weight of measured time, each week, month, and year went by, taking its toll of life and leaving in its place only the inconsistency of memories, and a veil of sadness and absurdity was lowered over human existence. On one of those numbered days, Lillith passed by there and was surprised not to see Adam plowing the field as was his custom. Without thinking, she peered through the window of his home and saw a hunchbacked, shrivelled old man, with a withered face and white hair, his eyes like two opaque marbles shedding tears and rheum, and a string of spittle hanging from a corner of his mouth. Out of the closed room came a penetrating stench of decomposing flesh, and, filled with anguish and resentment, she uttered for the second time the Ineffable Name.

"Who goes there?" muttered Adam, his eyes flicking back and forth, searching the infinity of his blindness. Seeing him chew the air with milky gums, Lillith fled, scattering behind her the shreds of an illusion that disintegrated like fog beaten by the wings of an apocalyptical hoot owl. She fled, haunted by the rotten smell that stuck in her nostrils and destroyed at once her memory of Adam and her vain hope for love.

Eve, sitting at the edge of her own death, heard Adam's question.

"It's probably the nocturnal ghost who is coming for my children."

"You don't have any children, Eve; they are all gone."

"Yes, I do. In the cradle, in the bed, at my breast, and in my womb I still have many children. I feel them; they pulsate inside me like larvae of hope because I have been a good mother, I have been a good woman, I have been a good wife. Do you still love me, Adam? Adam? Adam?!"

Eve . . . eternally

The one on this side
and the one on that side
cross the mirror
looking for each other
without knowing when they find the other
if they will be two times a body
or two times a reflection.

—Ulalume González de León

God, eager to create opposites and thus avoid eternal boredom, willingly accepted Sammaël's descent into the Abyss and took advantage of the opportunity to communicate to the Family of Man (as it came to be known because Woman was not paying attention) the existence of Evil, the Infernal Fires, and the King of Darkness. Thus He freed himself of the need to watch over human activities, attributing all future errors to the Other. Nevertheless, so as not to leave anything to chance, ever since the Fall it had seemed opportune to replace primary innocence with absolute ignorance, and, measuring human intelligence with a special micrometer, he calculated in light years the time it would take man to acquire knowledge and the infinitesimal possibility that that would happen. From then on He ceased to worry about earthly matters and all those petty problems that were driving him crazy.

While God carried out his Just Adjustments, the Earth

spun billions of times on its own axis and traveled millions of times around the Sun in an obsessive pattern only comparable to the vicious cycle of History. Adam and Eve and a thousand generations of their descendants went down the inevitable road to dust, and Sammaël came out of the Abyss.

When he emerged on the surface—and we have to say it like that, since his first impression was of being in the middle of a sea of enormous petrified waves—he realized how much time had elapsed since his Descent into the terrestrial intestines. And "he realized how much time" doesn't mean that he perceived it in lineal millennia, assigning a numerical value to something so abstract, as the members of the Family had done in order to measure the duration of their mortality, but rather he realized it the way someone would who returns to a place where he has left a seed and finds a forest. Sammaël had entered the Abyss through a crack in the middle of an extended, monotonous desert, and now he emerged through a cave in the highest peak of a vast expanse of volcanic mountain ranges. Stony pinnacles pierced the blue sky as far as the eye could see, as if a great celestial storm had liquified the earth's crust, bringing it to its maximum rebellion and then paralyzing it exactly at the moment when it was going to defy the laws of gravity.

Sammaël was profoundly moved by the brusque, petrified confusion of the landscape, the earth's cover piled on top of itself, cresting in peaks and spires, plummeting to the darkest depths and rising immediately to form new ridges. At his feet, in virginal unfolding, a blanket of the most immaculate snow spread down the mountain until it disappeared like delicate lace amid the trees that populated the lower slopes. The freezing wind continuously whipped the summit, making Sammaël's eyes cry. Between his tears and the snow's vaporous brilliance, Solitary Greeneyes glimpsed a simulacrum of the movement the mountain range still preserved, and he felt like a captain at the mast of a white ship in the midst of a tormented, immobilized sea. He was filled with the peculiar exaltation that comes with high altitude and imagined himself to be lord and master of all that he could see. He felt his soul expanding throughout the interminable landscape, until he abruptly collided with the deep pain of solitude repeated thousands of times in every crest, crevasse, cliff, slope, crater, canyon, ravine, promontory, and gorge. He remembered the purpose of his journey and thought he heard, in the beating of the wind, the whiplashing of metaphors he had dreamed and that had stuck relentlessly in his mind: "the golden honey of your lips," "the river of hair cascading down the slopes of your body," "the burning snow between your breasts," and for the third time, he set out in search of Eve . . . eternally.

Meanwhile, the Family of Man, following the Divine Mandate, was procreating, multiplying, and populating the Earth with the fruit of their wombs. The great-great-great-et cetera granddaughters of Eve gave birth in pain and sought their husbands with ardor and, according to some, let themselves be dominated, always wearing that malicious little smile that was on Eve's face so often while she was carrying out her domestic chores in Eden.

Consequently, the task that Sammaël had set for himself was both more and less difficult than he had imagined. He found not Eve, but thousands of reproductions with slight variations, all of them almost capable of replacing the original without being her exactly. He understood then that mortals, lacking the immortals' facility for transmigration of the soul, obsessively carry out a kind of transmigration of the flesh by means of a copious and unceasing reproduction that assures them of a relative and highly questionable immortality.

But the fervor that was produced in his mind and his heart

by the original hidden beneath all that variation blinded him to the reality of death and the impossibility of recovering his First Love, and he decided to search for it until he had exhausted all possibilities. Thus, by combining the experience of Brenda's Breasts, Thelma's Thighs, Fran's Face, Haley's Hair, Betty's Belly Button, Hanna's Hands, Lizzie's Lips, Wanda's Waist, and Leslie's Legs, which all successively drove him out of his mind in a copulatory frenzy of reconstruction, he managed to deceive himself for a while with the illusion that he finally had integrated the complete image of the woman he loved and therefore he had achieved satisfaction.

The only thing he really had achieved was exhaustion and the conviction that, besides dust, the other great constant in the Universe was frustration, and they both tasted the same. When he wanted to start all over again, he discovered that all of those women had developed a strange bulge in their belly that made it more difficult for him to get close. Since he had been the product of spontaneous generation, he was astonished by the dark, mysterious process of pregnancy and, deciding that paternity was something rather accidental and doubtful that had been thrust upon him in an unconditional way, he opted for leaving an endless trail of illegitimate children in the care of their respective mothers. So he began to wander through the Universe and through History with a definite taste of dust in his mouth and the infinite sadness of one who renounces forever an Unforgettable Illusion.

III Sammaël and Lillith

Beginnings and Endings

. . .there is no "one" truth, just a progressive, never definitive, liberation from errors.

—C. Coccioli, paraphrasing K.R. Popper

Having passed through the seven caverns of the Abyss and having learned everything there was to learn there; having passed, likewise, through the infinite daughters of Eve and having learned everything there was to learn there; and having passed, furthermore, through the most solitary solitude of absolute Orphanhood learning absolutely nothing, it was necessary—though doubtful—for Sammaël to encounter Lillith. Therefore, it was written since the Non-beginning of all time that Sammaël and Lillith would end up meeting, falling in love, and thus initiating The Still Incomplete Time after putting a Period at the end of contemporary history. The exact moment and place of their meeting depended entirely on chance.

God, indisputable Author of this chaotic and incredible story written without order on the white pages of the First Eternity, fought like a cat on his back to change the Ending. He re-wrote, erased, crossed out, changed the place and the chapter of important events, eliminated characters, and invented others, imbued everything with an indecipherable meaning to maintain suspense indefinitely, until He arrived at the sad but inevitable conclusion that endings are written long before beginnings and there is no Author of the World or in the world who can change them even a millionth of a point. It is possible that this admission cost God his health, and it is probable that Sammaël learned this simple lesson in the depths of the Abyss or the heights of Orgasm. Although it is also conceivable that he was completely unaware of it and his delay in showing up for the Date with Lillith was due to an existential lethargy that immortals experience during times of fog, because Sammaël with snail-like patience, wandered through space and the world, entering and exiting History and Its Unfolding, as Lillith was also doing, and thus these two predestined lovers did not find each other one second before chance had dictated their meeting.

Nevertheless, there was a fundamental difference. Even as the multiple names of Sammaël—Beezlebub, Asmodeus, Satan, Lucifer, Auld Clubfoot, and the Devil—were famous and infamous, as they were venerated, feared, rejected, adored, invented, cursed, and accused of almost everything that produces pleasure, distraction, or euphoria, Lillith's only name was more and more forgotten until it even ceased to be part of the stories grandmothers told on moonless nights. It did not appear, as did the Serpent's, in History or Mythology, or in witches' spells or oaths of faithful wives, or in the prayers of the trembling daughters of Eve. And Lillith, seeing herself drawn with the lines of silence and in the hues of oblivion, soon began to suffer a serious identity crisis. She understood then that it wasn't enough to know herself, to think herself, to feel herself, or to name herself; it wasn't even enough to see herself reflected on the surface of eternity. It was necessary to be able to measure herself in the words of others, to be materialized in the eyes of others, to be part of their fears or hopes, to be incorporated in myth and history, to be invented in everyday language or literature, to appear in philosophy and children's stories, in poetry and nightmares, to be part of lies and prayers and of our three-hundred-and-sixty-five daily breads in order to confirm her own existence.

Spiritually wounded, she had to admit that not one of her beautiful and unmistakable features was registered in the endless and varied annals of Man, not even as a dream or possibility. Her entrance into the world, her participation in historical events, her multiple seductions of well-endowed men, her intervention in individual destinies, and the practical jokes she played on good little girls had passed by so inadvertently that they weren't even registered in the rough drafts of oblivion. Lillith succumbed and began to wander—as Sammaël was doing, dragging his lost illusion behind him—with a mixture of indifference and resentment, along the margins of History, peeking over man's, the Serpent's and God's shoulders to catch a glimpse of reality, inferring the results of her distorted destiny by the elevated number of suicides, insane acts, and extreme cases of alcoholism among those females who deviated from the established Evian models.

She knew she had to wait, but she didn't know exactly what for, so she sat down on the edge of time and began to count the errors and horrors of History. She decided to take the exact measure of achievements, to calculate the proportion of disasters, to time successes, to appraise tragedies, cataclysms, and catastrophes; to weigh happiness, to prorate suffering, to gauge the perimeters of the rare islands of love, to calibrate the thickness of sorrow, the specific expanse of plenitude, and the interminable bulk of anguish, until she came to the conclusion that God was an Overgrown Child made in the Image and Likeness of Man, who in turn was made in the Image and Likeness of God, and that these two mutually dependent beings were subject to a reflection that was infinitely reversible. She began to perceive their multiple manifestations of pride and vanity, and she sensed in this immeasurable conceit, in this eternal mirroring in which God and Man contemplated each other, or invented each other, or strutted around pretending to be the Other, the seed of the First Mistake which, multiplied geometrically throughout History had produced such an unsolvable explosion of errors. And when she finally began to cry she saw mirrored on the surface of her tears, the exquisite reflection of Sammaël.

Of Brief and Unfathomable Things (1)

Delicate bird
I alight
on the branch
of your dense desire.
Butterfly,
I take flight
from the chrysalis
of your fire.

With the exact moment and place unascertained, the precise circumstances unknown, it is impossible to record the facts. Any conjecture, any hypothesis would lack scientific and historic validity. . .and, nevertheless. . .perhaps. . .we can imagine—blurry, almost inaccessible, enveloped in remnants of poetry—the precise moment in which Lillith's honey-colored eyes beheld Sammaël's dark Orphanhood and it penetrated to the womb of her own solitude. . .and the very instant, suspended in time, in which Sammaël's green eyes were invaded by Lillith's lucent Forsakenness and it pierced his abandonment. . .and we can imagine, along the fragmented margins of alienation, how, torn by a tearful tenderness, wrenched by the sweet cry of desire, Lillith tried to contain Sammaël's Orphanhood, and Sammaël tried to cover up Lillith's Forsakenness and, incredulous, each one pinned on the eyes, the tongue, the skin of the other; their bodies desperately investigated the possibility of occupying a single space, losing themselves in a mutual instant, in the obscure center of passion.

Of Brief and Unfathomable Things (II)

The memory of desire
is desire's own reflection,
just as the eye,
in recalling
sees itself.

With the exact moment and place unascertained, the precise circumstances unknown, it is impossible to record the facts. Any conjecture, any hypothesis would lack scientific and historic validity. . .

("Broken the night
that shelters my fire,
a liquid in flames
washes over me. . .")

. . .and, nevertheless. . .
perhaps. . .

we can imagine—
blurry,
almost inaccessible,
enveloped in remnants
of
poetry—

("the snail of my tongue
sketches

on your skin. . .
the precise moment

in which Lillith's honey-colored eyes beheld
Sammaël's dark Orphanhood
and it penetrated
to the womb of her own solitude. . .

. . .the trail
of its unctuous
inclination")

("Your wounded dove
alights
between my breasts")

and the very instant, suspended in time,
in which Sammaël's green eyes were invaded
by Lillith's lucent Forsakenness
and it
pierced
his abandonment. . .

("eager tunnel,
my body. . .

. . .the wings of sex,
a bat")

and we can imagine,
along the fragmented margins

("your mouth
in water born. . .") of alienation,

how,

torn by a tearful tenderness,
wrenched by the sweet cry of desire,

("the flavor of your sex
remained. . .

Lillith tried to contain Sammaël's Orphanhood,
and Sammaël tried to cover up Lillith's Forsakenness

. . .on my tongue,. . .
aroused")

on my tongue
always intense")

and, incredulous,
each one pinned on

("I sculpt. . .

the eyes,

. . .with my lips

the tongue,

the petals. . .

the skin

. . .of your incarnate rose")
of the other,

their bodies desperately investigated
the possibility
of occupying a single space,

("Delicate bird
I alight
on the branch
of your dense desire. . .

. . .Butterfly
I take flight
from the chrysalis
of your fire.)

losing themselves
in a mutual instant,
in the obscure center
of passion.

In Some Elliptical Angle of Infinity

And this is the way the world ends
And this is the way the world ends
And this is the way the world ends
Not with a bang but a whimper.
—T.S. Eliot

And God, tired of it all, gathered up his clouds and walked away. At that moment, the world was left bouncing like an abandoned ball on the solitary sidewalk of the Universe, enveloped in the abysmal silence that the human ear cannot stand, and man lost his image and his way, and in the 743 cardinal points of the Cosmos, not even the slightest whimper was registered, nor a minuscule trembling, nor an echo or a sob or a sigh to disturb the infinite stillness that had descended like a final curtain. And thus there was Absence, Total Absence, an infinite, absolute Absence in Itself. . .

A dense layer of foul-smelling smoke enveloped everything—thick, sticky, ocher-colored clouds. A dull, white tide paralyzed the waters of the seas. The leaves of the plants, the stems of the flowers, the petals of white daisies blackened and crackled as they were consumed in the invisible flames of Absence. An oily imminence covered the petrified face of the future, raising a howl of Dust in the middle of Nothing. Time stopped at the edge of the Void and History remained suspended, tremulous, in a definitive Twilight.

God had left and without even a slight chill to send him off. There was no cosmic storm, no eternal night, Heaven and Hell did not meet, nor was there a final conflagration; there was no uproar or shouting; there were only Absence and Hopelessness without end.

And then and only then, Lillith and Sammaël sought each other once more, they embraced once more in a limitless superposition of solitudes, and in that specific fraction of an instant, time was anchored exactly where parallel lines meet and planes are joined, where two bodies occupy the same space and immortality trembles with blinding brilliance for a matter of seconds. And then. . .

What no eye contemplated, no hand can record; what no mind understood, no word can explain; and what no being experienced can never belong to history.

And yet. . .

In some elliptical angle of infinity there began an incommensurable trembling that destroyed worlds and stars, reorganized entire universes and disintegrated others. It lasted a period of time that no one measured and when it ended, once again there was a silence beyond all silence. And then, in the middle of that interminable silence the fabric of time slowly began to tear, and to open the infinite darkness with a cosmic, intemporal scission through which—so it seems—a new god was being born.

MOZART DAY

Her delicate sensitivity, accustomed as it was to avoiding all unpleasantries including the thorns of roses, pricked its finger and bled bitterly. She watched as the thin thread of blood oozed over the surface of her happiness, relentlessly stained her complacent innocence, made obscene little drawings on the surface of her plenitude and headed straight for the front door of the house, seeped out onto the street, and finally trickled into the sewer, mixing with all the shit of the world. It was eleven in the morning. With a profound sigh, Mariana rolled up the transparent cloth of the day, gathered together the hours before her, and ran to lock herself in the bedroom.

Francisco arrived as usual at two o'clock, with peace in one pocket and hope in the other (not like the previous day when a sudden downpour had forced him to make an undignified dash to the door), expecting to find that cherished atmosphere of calm and well-being. He was surprised by the icy quiet. Upon hearing a subtle sigh hanging out of place in midair, he sensed the disengagement of something fragile in the filigree of time. Not only was he startled by Mariana's absence at the door, which could have been due to her elaborate creation of some culinary "Cézanne," but even more so by the subdued silence. In the kitchen the aromatic stillness of the pots steeped in exquisite spices and on the table the inexpressive eyes of the plates seemed to announce impending disaster. Then, there was the missing rose. A definite portent of a disrupted routine. The rose chosen daily by Mariana to be the focus of mesmerized contemplation in the center of the table, the one whose velvety reflections in the glittering hollows of the silverware reproduced to infinity the perfection of the chosen flower, was not there.

Francisco thought that possibly an inopportune butterfly had interrupted the cadence of morning hours or the silky song of a goldfinch could have frayed the lace of time, unraveling its continuity, but Mariana was not standing in the garden entranced by its beauty nor was she sitting at the edge of the open window. Broken pieces of morning were hanging in the air, fragments like disorderly sighs that hovered around the inexplicable void at the center of the table. There, exactly in the unseen umbilicus of that absence, hung the eleventh hour, the moment when Mariana entered more ephemeral and sensitive areas, after weaving the day's early threads onto the harmonious loom of morning colors. By eleven o'clock the house breathed the delicate aroma of bath salts, embroidered with the chiaroscuro of a precise perfume. The negligee with recherché ruffles rested draped behind the bathroom door and a small void in the huge closet announced the chromatic texture of the day: blue for tranquility, orange if there was a lot to do, green invited mischief, yellow spoke of internal sunshine, pink when she felt romantic, and beige for taking charge of the house. The multicolored pencils, paints, and powders had already invented a fresh look for her face, shaded here and there to bring out unexpected hues of the imagination.

Without a trace of vanity, Mariana would contemplate her image in the mirror, appreciating it through Francisco's eyes, feeling his slight shudder of pleasure as he noticed how the moss green of her dress flirted with the glaucous iridescence of her gaze. Only when she was completely satisfied did she descend the long staircase, opening the day before her step by step.

In the kitchen she toyed with Francisco's imagined hunger, searching for its nuances in a *picatta a la romana* (too strong for a yellow day); perhaps *coq au vin* (definitely pink); ah! *fruits de la mer au Pernod,* a taste of sun and sand. The words titillated her tastebuds while she gave detailed instructions (three teaspoons of *vin blanc,* a fourth of a teaspoon of Pernod), whose execution she would personally supervise (one more pinch of salt in the soup, Ramona, and the endives for the salad should be marinated in the vinaigrette for seventeen minutes before being served), and at one minute to eleven she headed toward the garden, allowing the culinary images to flow together with the frenzy of azaleas, daisies, and especially with the roses.

Nothing, absolutely nothing, as far as Francisco knew or could imagine, was capable of changing that moment to the slightest degree, almost the best of all the marvelous moments of the day, as Mariana had confessed to him, with the exception—of course!—of the moment when he arrived home. One full hour, belonging to her alone in the spacious garden behind the house (never the one in front, too close to the sounds, smells, and images of the world). The fresh tickling on the soles of her feet and in the spiral of the fleshy pink conch of her ear, the trilling of birds. The windows of her fingers opened to the silky petals of a flower, rainbow hues reflected on her face, exuding joy, hushed admiration, sudden dance, green air, fallen leaf, humid, absorbing the day, integrating herself into the world between blades of grass, face upward drunk with sun, flooded with multicolored light, pausing here, there, in front of the nostalgic wisteria, the perfect pansy, the tassled chrysanthemum, or the elegant yellow gilleyflower, until coming upon the rose, unique, an ornamental edging curled upon itself, hiding an ephemeral roundness of dew in its center. The hour in the garden was over. She would individualize the rose with her tiny silver scissors and place it in the delicate crystal holder exactly in the center of the table where at that moment Francisco contemplated its incomprehensible absence.

Bounding up the stairs two by two, he stopped abruptly at the closed door and knocked softly. Silence.

"Mariana? Mariana, are you there?. . . Mariana. Marianaaa!"

"Francisco, for God's sake! Don't be so tiresome," she answered without opening. "Leave me alone; I'm thinking."

Struck with hard, cold amazement, Francisco realized that things were worse than serious and possibly even irremediable. Mariana was thinking! Mariana, whose only thoughts blossomed at the edge of sensuality in all possible tones and who once said that the stubborn vice of reason was the cause of all human unhappiness.

"You think for me, Francisco," she had said. "Don't ask me to be rational or logical. You think for both of us. In exchange, I promise to create a home for you like no other, a miraculous cocoon, a chrysalis of light and warmth in which all the sorrows of the world will dissolve like zephyrs. There thought will be only a natural extension of the five senses and it will not need logical expression. Since the beginning of my life I have been taught to love beauty, to marvel at the senses, to weave the delicate filigree of each day in all its perfect sensuality, to be always happy and tender, to convert each moment into a wellspring of plenitude, touching it, savoring it, watching its most intimate expressions, and allowing myself to be caressed. But you must build me a safe haven where the world will never enter, with insurmountable walls that will isolate me from pain, suffering, knowledge, anguish, and the memory of death. There I will gather and store happiness and the pleasures of life to share them only with you."

And that's what he did. He enclosed Mariana in an impenetrable castle and filled it with plants and fish and birds and all kinds of flowers, works of art, and music. Within those tall, hermetic walls, he took pleasure with his wife like no man had taken pleasure with a woman since mythological times.

How could he understand that she had suddenly felt the diabolic need to think! He went down the steps one by one, surrounded by the sudden cracks and tears in that strange silence. It was supposed to be a Mozart day, Goddamnit!

Every day at his work he harbored the secret moment of returning home like a hidden promise, the thread of memory that would take him to the day's harmony that Mariana had announced that morning.

"This day feels like Bach, don't you think? Somber tones, clouds. . ."

"Mendelssohn, without a doubt, with that sun so yellow!. . ."

"A morning sigh demands a Mozart sonata. . ."

Thus, when he closed his office he sensed how their movements synchronized from a distance: He got into the car, she entered the study; he inserted the cassette in the tapeplayer, she placed the needle in the groove of the record. Entering through the front door was like picking up the melody of notes he had just left behind in the car. Only that last chord entered with him, nothing else; the world remained outside. And then. . . Mariana. Tender, smiling Mariana, beautiful Mariana, like a velvet breeze, devoted, docile, at the door with a kiss, a caress, taking his hand, weaving her fingers with his, never identical, always the same with unexpected variations, trembling and flush, inventing the day, soft and electric. They might make love between the soup and the second course or spend the entire meal with their little fingers gently intertwined, eat silently or fill the air with marvels and surprises; Mariana, joyful and prodigious.

"I found a twin leaf. Look! Look how the veins from one stem bifurcate. The delicate figuration makes me think of your hands. This morning the guppy gave birth. She filled the water with tiny black particles that suddenly blossomed heads and tails. The population in the fishtank is reaching dangerous levels. I sent for another one.

"Today I discovered the perfection of dust in a sparkling ray of sunshine painted on the transparency of the air. A perfect stroke of light, perforated by dust particles as if they were needle points. There, in suspension, equidistant from each other, until I breathed and they scattered, colliding, falling, vanishing into the infinite space of shadows. When you and I are dust, my love. . ."

She always seemed to know his needs before he arrived, and to prepare the perfect remedy. Mariana the diviner, Mariana the magician, Mariana. . . thinking?

The confinement lasted three days and nights while the rose that should have been cut that Mozart Tuesday lost its petals in natural solitude without ever having reached the dignity of individualization on the white tablecloth. Daily activities in the house stuttered to a halt. Francisco called in sick and consumed his hours and the carpet in a tireless pacing up and down between the living room and the bedroom door. The rhythm of domestic chores degenerated into an irregularity of false starts until it stopped completely and Ramona stagnated at meatballs and beans twice a day. The canaries lost their feathers and the guppy gulped down her twenty-four offspring without gaining a milligram. Everything seemed to shrink and pine in response to the assault of meatballs and Mariana's absence. Only the silence thickened until it was dense and opaque.

At two in the afternoon of the third day the bedroom door opened, and Mariana, dressed in a somber gray suit and street shoes, with no makeup and with her dull hair pulled back severely at the nape of her neck, descended the stairs to the dining room, sat at the table and began to eat the three cold meatballs that Ramona had carefully left at her place just in case. When Ramona saw that, she turned beet red and covered her mouth with her hand.

"Meatballs, Ramona, are delicious and very nutritious. We should eat them more often," were her first words. "And if you're going to cry, please do me the favor of doing it in your own room and not here while I'm eating."

"Mariana. . ."

"Don't whine, Francisco, it's not the end of the world. Actually, it's very simple. It entered; now it's here, everywhere, in the corners, around the table, behind the door. I don't know how it snuck in. There must be a crack, a little opening, perhaps a loose tile or a split in the caulking around a window; I don't know. I looked for it; I swear to you. I looked for it like crazy all Tuesday morning, on my knees I peered under every door, I checked the edges of the windows, I examined the wall inch by inch, I inspected the ceiling, but I didn't find anything. If I had found a crack I would have covered it; I thought there was still time, that it would be just a minimal shadow, a sigh that once isolated inside would dissipate. It was hopeless. I was enveloped by lamentations, I penetrated the shadow, I felt the nostalgia of crying and then the pain of the world, so infinite and interminable that I ran, frightened, to shield myself behind the closed door of the bedroom. I covered my ears, I closed my eyes, but it had already adhered to my skin, sticking to my tongue, nestling in my gut as if I were about to give birth. Then I understood the dry indifference of the rose, the ancestral hunger of fish, the bitter song of canaries in captivity, the solitude of plants, and the cruelty of rain. I saw the possibilities of dust and I knew why Ramona's eyes are dark and why they suffer sudden shadows of forgetfulness. I understood that memories inhabit our sighs and I asked myself why silence is the last possible dream on earth. There's no going back."

Francisco realized that any gesture on his part would constitute a farewell and he took refuge in a confused acceptance, a present without questions, and an endless waiting.

Just a few days after Mariana had left, Ramona was cleaning the house when she found among the thick folds of the rug at the entranceway a tiny lump of mud, probably fallen from some hasty shoe on the day of the sudden downpour.

IN MEMORIAM

hymen. *[LL, from the Greek hymen, membrane]: a fold of mucous membrane partly closing the orifice of the vagina while maintaining its integrity. —Taken from Diccionario de la Lengua Española, Real Academia Española, Ed. XIX*

Whatever has been lost usually remains in the last place you left it and is found in the last place you look, so what I lost is probably still in that sordid pay-by-the-hour motel near the beach, because I never went back for it. Frankly, it wasn't any good to me before or afterward, and that business about "integrity" is a mystery because no part of me disintegrated. I would have preferred, of course, to have lost it on a solitary, moonlit beach, rocking to the sound of passionate waves, or in a cluttered, artistic bachelor's pad among reams of amorous poetry, or under a luxuriant tree in a soft bed of leaves, with a late-afternoon sun streaking down through the foliage, in order to embellish my memory with a certain romantic flair, but the cards fall where the cards fall and you can't always choose.

Neither can I adorn my story with impassioned obfuscation or with an unexpected moment of weakness, because we both knew perfectly well, even though we didn't say so, why we were going to that faraway beach or he wouldn't have taken a bottle of tequila and I a blanket.

John belonged to that inevitable series of awkward, fervent romances in every normal adolescence, complete with skirmishes in the back seat of his car, kisses so prolonged that we almost suffocated, shyness and insecurity that stirred up a passion beyond all reason, dreams, illusions, and plans for a future that was fortunately quite distant and nebulous. But we believed we loved each other and, for some unfathomable reason, we both sensed that the time had come to cast off fears and shame and become adults.

I think I told my parents about going to the beach, omitting the fact that we would be alone. I remember that we drove in silence, each of us lost in our own thoughts and doubts. It didn't occur to me that he was afraid because I didn't want to think about that, and I wasn't feeling much either because I had put out of my mind any notion of what we were going to do. I was headed for the beach armed with pure, virginal innocence. We women, I believe, have the innate ability to feel ourselves seduced beyond our power of resistance at the slightest provocation, or to commit an act of free will without assuming any responsibility for it. It's a question of survival. I, for one, had no trouble packing into the same mental suitcase a trembling enthusiasm and the firm conviction that I was being led to the slaughterhouse, and it was useless to resist. That all had to do with the vagaries of my upbringing and education.

I downed two tequilas to shore up my courage, tuned the radio to the latest hits, and tried not to worry about the only thing that really worried me: what John would think of me afterward.

When we got to the beach, we stopped the car, took the

blanket and the tequila, and walked a way until finding an ideal spot where we could admire sea, sky, and palm trees at the same time without having to raise our heads. It was a silent conspiracy to turn the commonplace into something memorable. We spread the blanket over the warm sand, beneath a moon that should have been unforgettable but that I can't remember, and we sat down with another shot of tequila for our nerves. It occurred to me that it would be appropriate to demand a promise of marriage—in the future, of course—but I desisted out of fear that he would agree and that would create problems in the long run. Instead, I adorned my seduction a bit with the conventional phrase, "I love you," even though I wasn't quite sure about that, except when we were apart and there was enough distance between us to fantasize.

He lay me down on the blanket and began to kiss me with his usual awkwardness. I went completely limp: I didn't want him to misinterpret the slightest movement as cooperation. I don't remember feeling anything; there was no excitement, no desire, nothing. I was too busy feeling like a passive victim of a situation from which it was too late to escape, and struggling to believe it. I remembered all the stories we women tell each other about the terrible testicular cramps that men suffer due to sudden frustration and I decided to sacrifice myself for poor John, who was not to blame for his irrepressible urges.

We were making progress. He caressed my breasts and genitals while I emitted gentle whimpers to convince him that I was beyond good and evil, with my will totally vanquished. The last thing I remember was the weight of his body on mine, both of us still dressed, and the surprising sensation of his erect penis between my legs. I felt faint, I couldn't breathe, and at that very moment an enormous wave unleashed all of its salty fury on us. We leapt up, coughing sand and dripping water from head to toe. The bottle of tequila had taken to sea;

the blanket was full of tiny crabs, surprised to find themselves on such a soggy nuptial bed, and John and I looked at each other with frustration and relief.

It should have ended there, and if we had enjoyed a sense of humor, we would have had a good laugh, accepting the tragicomic ending to our endeavor and postponing the consummation for a more propitious and less damp date. But it was September and I was eighteen and Elvis Presley was singing "It's Now or Never," so when John asked if we should go to a motel and continue, I ignored his interrogative tone and accepted what he proposed as an irrevocable order, proving once again that we women are always victims of circumstance because our mothers never prepared us for anything.

With my silence as consent, we arrived at a raunchy motel whose entrance—a dark, obscene passageway—was only a few yards from the hustle and blinding lights of the main strip. John made me hunch down in the front seat, I suppose to protect my honor, but he only managed to destroy my last shred of dampened dignity as he haggled with the night manager, who finally agreed to let us have a room until three in the morning, for ten dollars. I felt my virginity had been bartered away for a miserly price, and feared my initiation—already public knowledge—would become a masturbatory fantasy for all the hotel's shadowy employees.

The room, with unmistakable signs of innumerable transitory nights, had shabby brown walls and a shameless orange bedspread that for some mysterious reason made me feel like the tragic heroine of a third rate movie, but I didn't say anything because it was already too late, and by then money had changed hands. At least the sheets seemed clean, but the sand had been a princess's bed compared to the hills and valleys of the mattress. With a shudder, I lay down on the rancid memories of other bodies.

We had started to go at it when I suddenly remembered that we couldn't continue. I felt a wave of relief and a little guilt for John's frustration.

"John! What if I get pregnant?"

He looked at me with feverish eyes and, shaking with disbelief, got up and reached for his pants. I was just about to look for my stockings when I saw him take out his wallet and remove a small white packet. Horrified, I watched him open the packet, take out a wet, translucent object and pull it over his erect penis. I wanted to die. How could he have been so cold, so calculating, so prepared, and so dispassionate as to have bought that disgusting thing beforehand?! I hated him; I knew I was doomed and I gave in to the inevitable.

So it all went as it had to and I, well, I barely felt anything. Of course, in those days I was expecting the San Francisco earthquake. What I did experience was surprise. I took advantage of John's trip to the bathroom to look at the sheets and I was amazed to find the historical and hysterical red stains. So it was true! I had never been convinced by the stories of the hymen or the test of the sheets to prove or disprove virginity. That had all seemed like old wives' tales to scare restless young girls. But no: There were the bloody remains of what was lost, that presence in absence felt, silent testimony to what had been, and suddenly I thought I should cry. Not that I wanted to, but it seemed like the appropriate thing to do. Actually, I felt very calm, a little disillusioned by the utter insignificance of it all, but quite serene. And in some back corner of my conscience, being tranquil was equivalent to being a slut, so I broke into such wrenching sobs that John came running over to hug me and swear that he would never do again that which had produced so much suffering and so little pleasure. By the repentant tone of his voice, I knew that my reaction had been suitable to save in his mind the last vestiges of my doubtful decency, and I kept crying for a while longer.

I let him pamper me the whole way back to my house and we ended the night by swearing eternal love and painting our future in platonic hues of pink. I went up to my room, slipped between the immaculate, fresh sheets, and fell asleep immediately. The next morning I opened my eyes and thought: I'm not a virgin any more. I waited. Nothing. No change, no emotion, no euphoria, not even guilt. I shrugged my shoulders, put on my bathing suit, and went for a swim.

OF CHEESE AND CHRIST

Some people arrived at the conclusion
that dreams were caused by devils;
others, that they came from divinities. They
explained dreams as memories of the human
soul, which wandered around separate from the body
during sleep; as messages from dead relatives;
as pure and creative fantasies; even
as the ordering by the mind
during sleep of recent events.

(The Sacred Dream)

Right now I couldn't say for sure if it was a dream or reality, or both, but I remember it as if it really happened and so that's the way I'll tell it. I know it left a mark as clearly as any concrete event in my life, and that makes me think that perhaps there's not much difference between dreams and waking life, anyway.

It happened at my aunt's house, the fussy one we didn't like. Everything bothered her, like the time my mother left an unwrapped slice of onion in the refrigerator and upon discovering it she started complaining in a loud voice that the whole mess stank to high heaven and thanks to her sister-in-law's carelessness she now would have to throw away a lot of good food.

In my opinion, that was an exaggeration; after all, we eat onions, both raw and cooked, and my aunt had a refrigerator stuffed so full of food, half of it spoiled, that it needed a good cleaning anyhow. The unwrapped onion was just an excuse to make my mother clean the refrigerator. Seeing her do it made me angrier than my aunt's unfair accusations: She tensed her jaw and lowered her eyes to hide her rage, but she cleaned it thoroughly. I knew that would ruin the rest of her day, and surely my brother and I would suffer for it. I never understood why my mother was so afraid of her sister-in-law and, being so afraid, why we always ended up depending on my aunt's less-than-gracious hospitality. But there we were, putting up with every indignity because my father, who was an architect, hadn't finished fixing up the small house he had bought for us, and we didn't have any place to live.

Sometimes my mother took it out on my father instead of on us. As soon as he arrived, she'd start yelling at him: Why wasn't the house finished? Why was he late? Why did she have to put up with his sister's attacks? I'd keep very still and not say anything, but deep down I believed my aunt and my mother were more alike than either one would admit.

But what I want to tell you about is the day of the cheese and Christ, because that day changed our lives, the kind of significant change that literature is about, not just a little sad or a little comical like the daily problems with onions and my parents' love spats. They did love each other, I'm sure of that; always after a quarrel, once the insults and divorce threats had died down, they had reconciliations behind closed doors while my brother and I watched television.

On the day in question, my aunt left early for the city. I think she was going to home-decorating class or something like that. We knew she wouldn't be back all day because once downtown she would go to the beauty parlor and then eat with her friends in some "luxuuuuuurious" restaurant, as my mother said, or "at least that's what she claimed," commented my mother with a little smirk. As soon as my aunt was gone, my mother became angry.

"She didn't even say good-bye, or leave food made or instructions about what we should or shouldn't eat. . . Nothing! It's a trap!" she grumbled as soon as she heard the door slam. For her there was no doubt that whatever we touched in the refrigerator would set off a new round of reproaches by her sister-in-law. "Well, she'll see: We won't eat anything!"

The nutritional prospects were dim. My brother and I had only had juice and bread with jam for breakfast because my aunt didn't have children and she was on a never-ending diet that didn't include breakfast. There wasn't even butter for our bread, much less eggs.

"I can't believe what you feed your kids!" she had exclaimed one morning in which my mother had made us a complete breakfast. "You could give them rat poison and they would be healthier!"

And so she stopped buying everything that had cholesterol—including milk, eggs and butter—and we stopped eating breakfast. That was when lowering cholesterol consumption was the latest fad, and, since my aunt followed all the fads and imposed her most recent opinion on everyone under her control, we had to de-cholesterolize ourselves. That's how she was about everything: According to her, you had to buy clothes in certain stores, preferably in Paris, dine in certain restaurants in vogue, eat a certain way, which was the way she did at the moment, or you were a country bumpkin. My mother and brother and I were country bumpkins, of course, although she never messed with my father, which made my mother even more furious.

Well, as I said, my mother decided that we wouldn't eat anything that day, thus hoping to make my aunt feel guilty, but she could have saved herself the trouble because I'm sure that we would have died before my aunt felt the slightest twinge of guilt.

As soon as we were informed of the fast that awaited us, my brother and I ran to the pantry and stealthily began to extract cookies and crackers from open boxes, closing them afterwards very carefully so the pilferage wouldn't be detected. We put our loot under the bed so we could eat it little by little as the long, drawn-out day progressed.

The day proceeded as we expected, with no possible salvation; boiling inside because of the injustice, my mother yelled at us for anything we did, or for not doing anything. All morning long she was like a madwoman: She insulted our aunt at the top of her voice, or she seethed in a voiceless rage, like a stubborn goat, losing what little patience she had. I think she was fed up with us. I was glad my father wasn't there because she surely would have thrown him out for good. At least she couldn't throw us out, or kill us, so we knew that all we had to do was put up with it and in the end she would go back to being normal. The hours were exhausted either by escaping to the back yard to get out of her way and being scolded for laziness, or by trying to help and being scolded for getting in the way.

It was twelve o'clock and my brother was howling because of a whack on the head he had earned by not smoothing all the wrinkles out of the bed, when the mailman arrived. I heard the bell ring and ran to open the door so I wouldn't be included in the punishment. The mailman smiled at me and said "good morning"—which I'm sure it was for him, although not for us, because we hadn't eaten anything, not even the cookies hidden under the bed that my mother had found and confiscated—and he handed me several white envelopes and one large manila one.

I put them all on the front table and was just about to go out to the yard when my mother came out of her room and began to check the mail as if she were expecting something. She made some sarcastic comments about the bills my uncle would have to pay because of my aunt's unreasonable spending, and left the white envelopes where I had put them. But the manila one—to my surprise—she carried to the living room and, sitting down on the peach-colored sofa, she put her feet up and began to open it, just like that. Now, allow me to explain the seriousness of this series of transgressions, committed with the greatest disdain I have ever seen in my mother. First of all, entering the living room was forbidden; sitting on the sofa—and putting up her feet! Well, that was unthinkable, and without taking off her shoes! made her a candidate for the firing squad. But nevertheless, there was my mother, carefree as can be. My brother and I observed her from the doorway as she opened the envelope, took out a magazine, looked at it, and let loose an exclamation of glee and then a shrill, vengeful laugh. Suddenly, kissing and hugging the magazine, she looked up, and discovered us standing there, astonished. She gestured for us to come near.

I was so surprised that I even forgot my hunger. Fearfully, we took off our shoes and, tiptoeing so we wouldn't mark the thick carpet, went to sit one on either side of our mother.

The magazine had pictures of luxurious homes and gardens, with beautiful photographs in full color of the most stunning houses in the country. It was a magazine that my aunt treasured, and she tried to emulate each one of the fine details of the most opulent mansions that were pictured there.

Ever since she had subscribed to the publication, my aunt liked to compare her own house, decorated with textiles imported from Italy and custom-made Chinese rugs, with the competition's photos, in order to prove to herself that she had better taste than anybody else. A few months ago—our mother explained to us with obvious delight—our aunt had met the editor of the magazine at a party and she had suggested to him that there were several houses in her neighborhood worthy of being featured, including hers, of course. The editor had sent reporters and photographers to canvass the area and they had photographed three or four of the most luxurious houses, including my aunt's. From that moment on, she had announced to all who would listen that soon her house would be on the cover of the magazine in question and had waited anxiously for the corresponding number to arrive so she could show off to the neighbors, whom my aunt hated because she suspected that they had more money than she and our uncle did.

My mother let out another belly laugh of pure pleasure, and she pointed to the color photos of the neighbors' house. Since my brother didn't know how to read yet, I read the caption out loud, "House of the month: The Spencers," and underneath there was a photograph with the smiling neighbors in front of the honored house. In the background, we could barely see the silhouette of my aunt's house. My mother broke out laughing again and hugged us with ferocious joy, which seemed so strange and unfamiliar that it gave me a chill.

"She's going to be so mad she'll burst!" she exclaimed, laughing and rocking back and forth with pleasure. "She's going to die of envy!" In a loud, mocking voice she read the magazine's praise of Mrs. Spencer's impeccable taste with regard to the decoration of every corner of her house, and she kept hugging us over and over. I remember that her closeness made me anxious instead of relieved, and I was almost grateful when she finally let us go.

"I'm famished!" she exclaimed. "Let's get something to eat."

I was so overjoyed to hear those words that I jumped off the sofa and ran to the kitchen, remembering—and the image had tortured me all morning as my hunger intensified—that last night I had seen at least seven big portions of recently purchased cheeses in the refrigerator. Nevertheless, when I opened the door, the shelf where I thought I had seen them was empty. I felt a nauseating emptiness in my stomach as I contemplated the sad, withered remains of a few vegetables and three slices of ham, slightly green around the edges. I thought perhaps my aunt, to keep us from eating, had taken all the food with her this morning and I hated her more than ever. Now, with the time that has passed, I think that maybe I dreamed the full refrigerator and what I found was reality, or I dreamed the empty refrigerator and everything else, too. Memory is tricky, not at all reliable. I realize today that my aunt probably wasn't as cruel, nor my mother so vengeful as my memories of them. Or perhaps they were just as I recall.

But what does come to mind quite clearly is when my mother found an unopened cheese in a drawer of the refrigerator. It was Camembert and it was just ripe for eating—that's what my mother said, almost lustfully—and it had that semi-rotten smell that my father had taught me to appreciate in good, mature cheese, and a creamy, appetizing consistency.

Eating that cheese was, at once, the greatest temptation, and the gravest effrontery that my mother ever committed—and my brother and I with her—in my aunt's house. It was obvious that it was being saved for a special occasion, since it wasn't even opened, and it was also obvious that the occasion was near because the cheese was just right. But my mother's euphoria and our hunger were even more obvious, and more powerful.

We cut the fancy cover off the cheese, found some crackers imported from Sweden that went well with it, and, laughing and chattering, ate the whole thing. My mother even dared open a bottle of good French wine and serve us a glass diluted with water "just to celebrate," she said. When we finished there was nothing left of the cheese, the crackers, or the wine; just crumbs and empty glasses. With my stomach full, I started to fear what my aunt would do when she discovered our transgression, but the fear didn't last long before it melted into a delicious desire to sleep.

That's where my memory becomes a bit muddled, and I'm not sure if we had just arisen from our nap or if we were on our way to the bedroom to sleep when the Christ thing happened. What I do remember is the surprise I felt upon discovering that in the vestibule we passed through on our way to the bedroom, there was an enormous glass showcase I had never noticed before, that covered the whole wall. Now I think I probably had seen it all along, but had forgotten about it. Inside the case was a figure of Christ, larger than life, dressed in a purple tunic edged with pure gold thread that came down to his bare feet. The tunic was tied at the waist with a golden sash. The Christ figure appeared in profile, in front of an enormous rock or boulder that he seemed just about to climb. He had his hands placed high on the rock as far as he could reach and he had raised his left foot, as if he were going to pull himself up at any moment. Now that I think about it, that's a strange position for Christ, who is almost always on his cross, or in Mary's lap, or with his hand extended, giving a blessing. His face was turned upward as if he could see something above the rock that the outside observer couldn't; he had a grave expression on his face, like great concentration, or deep pain. What that Christ was doing in the entrance to the house when my aunt professed no religion, I've never been able to explain and never dared ask because of what happened next. Perhaps my memory deceives me, for now I understand that childhood is an eternal invention, fabricated in the adult mind. But I promised to tell the story just as I remember it.

As I said before, I don't recall if we were coming from or going to our room, but my mother, my brother, and I stopped in front of the Christ figure, gazing at him as if we saw him for the first time. There was a moment of silence more intense than our guilt over the cheese we had just eaten, and then my mother approached the access door on the side of the case, probably used for cleaning or taking out the Christ when necessary. She moved slowly, almost like in a dream. She opened the door and entered the glass case. I felt afraid, but couldn't move or speak; I remember the sensation clearly as my mother stood behind the Christ figure, looking at his straining back, arched as if he were just about to climb the boulder. Then the Christ lowered his raised foot, took his hands from the rock and slowly turned to face my mother. He looked at her with a tenderness I had never seen before—not even in my father's eyes when they kissed—and I've never seen again, and then he smiled. It was a smile both sad and sweet. She looked back at him, and her face looked almost childlike, filled with a luminous wonderment. She was transfigured. I thought I should be afraid for her, but before such a loving gaze it was impossible to feel fear. I stood very still, astonished, and without missing a single detail.

The Christ extended his enormous hand and lay it gently on my mother's still-blonde hair; they looked at each other with eyes so full of tenderness, love, and happiness that I had to close mine. When I opened them again, the Christ had withdrawn his hand and my mother's countenance was full of light; a smile spread over her whole face. At that instant and before my very eyes, the Christ figure dissolved, as if melted by the heat of my mother's smile, disappearing slowly like ice over fire, and the purple tunic crumpled gracefully, in a subtle dance that reduced it to a mound of fabric on the floor of the glass showcase. My mother stood alone in the case, with all the happiness in the world on her face. I suddenly realized that I loved her, more than any other human being in the world or beyond it, and how I would never be capable of expressing or demonstrating to her the enormity of that love.

The next day, or perhaps a few days later, we moved into our own home. I don't remember if my aunt was angry about the cheese; perhaps she arrived while I was asleep and I didn't hear her shouting, but I don't have any particular memory of her reaction.

My mother went back to being the same person she had always been and I never saw her again as that blessed angel who appeared in the showcase. But that one vision had made me understand forever that my mother was and always would be the purest love of my life. The next time we visited my aunt's house, one Sunday, I looked for the glass case that should have been empty, but I only found a solid wall that exhibited a huge abstract painting with violent yellow and purple colors. Nobody spoke of a missing Christ figure, and I understood that asking impertinent questions about Christs or cheeses that might have disappeared on a certain long gone afternoon could possibly make all the wrath of God and of my family descend upon my head.

BALZAC

They bought him to fill an incipient menopausal void in their marriage and because he had long, floppy ears. A melancholy look with red, droopy eyelids and short crooked legs befitted his deformed but adorable breed. A twinge of literary nostalgia suggested the name.

As a puppy he filled their house with tenderness and play, sprinkled the rugs with pee, and left hair on the legs of their pants. But like doting grandparents, they tolerated everything. Then, one day, Balzac reached juvenescence and his mischievous cavorting degenerated into a perennial state of exaltation that bordered on insanity. His owners, having long forgotten the power of instinct, were horrified as they contemplated Balzac's wild, erotic contortions while he desperately searched for satisfaction with any object that could support his weight. The elderly couple dusted off old memories of their own adolescent offspring and concluded that the dog's excitement would simmer down by itself once he got through this conflictive stage. In an effort to calm the bewitched creature, they took advantage of his every exhausted moment to reward him with platonic caresses on his ears and belly. Far from soothing the fiery Balzac, this innocent petting set off increasingly frenetic searches for a female that deteriorated into frantic racing around the garden and hopeless attempts to squeeze his furry body under the front gate. This canine frenzy eventually destroyed the garden and was just about to cause irreparable damage to the couple's tranquil marriage when Balzac discovered the bucket. It was a beautiful blue bucket made of pliable but firm plastic with a brass handle, bought on clearance because it was slightly taller and narrower than normal. During the day it was used for soaking clothes, and at night it served to sublimate Balzac's boundless erotic energy. The gentle curve of the bucket's torso, the soft resistance of the plastic, the fact that when lying down it was perfectly mountable, all seemed to the delirious male to be unmistakably feminine characteristics. He never contemplated the problematic color blue or the awkwardness of a litter of buckets with floppy ears.

All day he prowled the back patio, stalking the slender pail, frustrated by her erect position and the abundant soapy water that impeded all contact. He lost his appetite when the alluring bucket reacted with cold indifference to the insinuating wags of his tail. He became gaunt and soon substituted his wild dashes around the garden for a supine, expectant position in the back patio, watching every irresistible movement of the blue seductress. The couple observed the dog's new stillness and believed his adolescence was over. The household returned to its comfortable routine.

In the back patio Balzac learned to wait for nightfall in quiet desperation, alternating cold sweats with flashes of heat, or trembling as he endured the agony of a slow simmer. Sometimes he had to drop suddenly to his belly in order to hide a telltale erection when he saw the maid lifting and lowering the beloved bucket, plunging her arms down into it, inserting and extracting clothes, or thoughtlessly running her hands over its curvaceous exterior. In the light of day there was nothing he could do. But in the evening the bucket was emptied and placed upside down to dry. Balzac would endure increasing tension as he waited for the precise moment when the lights of the house would be turned off, so he could approach the object of his desire. Then, he would slowly lick her from top to bottom in order to erase the memory of detergent and to soften her resolve. Although he managed to knock her over on her side with a playful little shove of his nose, the mischievous pail would roll out from under his impassioned paws. Then he would try to seize her tenderly and once more she would roll away. And so the game continued: the flirtatious bucket escaping from beneath the floppy-eared suiter's amorous advances, rolling around and around, scarcely allowing Balzac the pleasure of licking what he saw as the fulfillment of his desires. Finally, the panting dog would manage to drag her to a flat place in the patio and mount her with desperate spasms until she rolled out from under him, throwing him down on the cold concrete. Then Balzac's frustration, demanding cooperation and tenderness, would erupt in virile barks which echoed in the cold, hollow torso of the beloved pail. The incessant flirtatiousness of the pliable plastic provoked renewed erotic efforts by the would-be lover, but the bucket put up such dogged resistance to penetration that Balzac felt his sanity dissolving in a sea of unrequited desire.

One dark night of overwhelming desperation Balzac's endurance snapped and he attacked the beloved blue skin with his fangs amid heartwrenching howls that alarmed the entire neighborhood, until the plastic pieces of passion lay scattered beneath his feet. A week later the couple had to call a veterinarian to put the poor animal to sleep forever in order to silence the unbearable wailing and retrieve the brass handle of the shredded bucket which he guarded jealously in a dark corner of the doghouse.

EARL

That was his name. Since then I haven't met anyone else with that name. He was my first love, after my father, of course, and a cousin; I guess that makes him my first non-incestuous love. Earl. I remember him—and this could be a betrayal of the truth like most memories—as quite handsome: tall and slender with straight, black hair, combed back and held in place with gel. That's how my father's hair was: black, straight, combed back with Wildroot that had a slight aroma of perfume and left his hair as fine as silk, lying comfortably against his head without grease or goo. I still recall the satin-like sensation of my father's hair when I caressed it. In my memory, that's the impression I have of Earl's hair, just like my father's: silky, clean, smelling vaguely of Wildroot. Earl's eyes, unlike my father's, which were blue, were large and black, framed with long, seductive eyelashes. My father, on the other hand, scarcely seemed to have any lashes at all, they were so short, and he had deep eyes, neither big nor small, with a merry—perhaps mischievous—twinkle. That was one of the things that always surprised me about my dad: his capacity for joy in spite of the problems he'd had. He loved life, and he drank it down in great gulps, with unusual pleasure. I've always wanted to learn how to be that way, but it hasn't been easy. Anyway, Earl fascinated me. We were in the same Spanish class in sixth grade. It was my last year in grade school and I felt big and important; I could boss other kids around, the little ones in the lower grades. I wasn't thinking about the next year when I would start over again in the lowest grade of junior high. I enjoyed being the know-it-all of primary school, together—of course—with the rest of my classmates.

Earl always sat in back with his buddies, Ralph and Thomas. I was in the second row, four ahead of Earl, but on the same side of the classroom. Once in a while I heard him joke with his friends, answer a question, or make a comment. It was as if my ears were attuned to the exact tone of his voice, like those of a dog who recognizes without a doubt the motor of his master's car when it's still a block away from home. When class was over, I always stood up quickly to turn toward him before he left the room, not so he would look at me, but just to let my eyes rest on the back of his neck, his shoulders, his waist, his hips, his legs, or any other part of his body, and feel myself falling inward with unexpressed love, an emotion of both pleasure and pain, yearning and fearing. He rarely noticed my gaze because he was always flanked by his two inseparable buddies. Nevertheless, every once in a while he would glance back at the class as he left the room, or he wouldn't have started to leave yet when I turned to contemplate him, and then our eyes would meet briefly in the instant before I lowered mine and pretended to be busy gathering my books.

I had only one friend, Emilia. She was short, chubby, homely, and unpopular, and I think that's why I liked her: She needed me more than I felt I needed her. Now I understand that needs are two-way streets, and they flow in both directions without distinguishing between intensities or degrees. Nonetheless, hanging out with Emilia made me feel less fat, homely, and unpopular than I felt when I was alone. I know now that almost all thirteen-year-old girls feel fat (or too skinny), homely, and unpopular, but back then that notion couldn't hold any truth for me because Susan—who was blonde with blue eyes, just like me—seemed to be sure she was the prettiest and most popular girl in the sixth grade, and she always was surrounded by most of the desirable boys, as well as almost all of the girls who didn't seem to feel as badly about themselves as I did. Anyway, I think that part of the problem was that my mother was the most beautiful woman in the world and she knew it and everybody around her knew it, too. My grandmother said that her daughter was so beautiful that she, my grandmother, spent all of her life enraptured by her beauty. In contrast, she used to say to me, "round face, round mouth, round eyes," and even though she said it affectionately I always felt that her description was a little derogatory. I was never able to compete with my mother's beauty and have finally accepted the fact that I have my own attractiveness, especially inside, and that I don't have to compete. But at thirteen, I felt defeated in an unfair battle that I would have preferred to avoid but that was imposed on me from birth, and this defeat humiliated me so terribly that it was difficult to appreciate any physical quality that I might have. I decided to develop my mind and ignore my body, but when you're thirteen and you start liking boys, your mind isn't worth beans and you're stuck with your body image whether you like it or not. So I was in love with Earl, but I never thought that he could be interested in me.

Emilia didn't understand what I saw in Earl. She said he was ugly, too skinny and—what was worse—somewhat dark-skinned. She preferred Sam, a pale little guy from El Paso who spoke with an obnoxious Texan accent, and she applauded everything he said as if it were quite interesting and important. But Sam didn't look at all like my father and there was no way that I could find him attractive. I convinced myself that Emilia was jealous because I was in love and she wasn't. That was obvious because she didn't spend all the hours of Spanish class dreaming and sighing listlessly, as I did every time I thought of Earl.

I remember fantasizing tirelessly every night that I would become gravely ill before the end of the school year and the teacher would announce it in class. On the spot, Earl would realize that he had always been crazy in love with me and finally, threatened with losing forever the love of his life, he would run to my side, kneel down, and beg me not to die. With the fantasy my soul filled with joy, my undies became deliciously and sinfully damp, and I debated between ending it by dying in his arms and leaving him to mourn for the rest of his life or healing because of his love and living happily ever after, idolized by the man of my dreams. Most of the time I fell asleep before deciding, right in the heat of the most exciting moment when we were embracing each other, burning with love, and just as I was filled with sensations that I never described to Emilia because I was certain she would be horrified, as would my parents, teachers, and everyone else.

Three weeks after I had first discovered this passionate and endless love for Earl, the long-awaited and unavoidable end of the school year arrived. I remember my surprise when Susan invited me to her party to celebrate our "graduation," and my guilty feeling when I heard that Emilia was not to be invited. I had to lie when my best friend asked me to spend the night at her house on the same Saturday as the party and I thought that if she ever found out my betrayal, she would end our friendship forever. And, just as I suspected, a short while after we had hung up—with my apologizing more than necessary for not being able to go to her house because my mother had punished me for not cleaning my room—another classmate, called "Four Eyes" because of her bottle-bottom glasses, had called Emilia to ask if she was going to Susan's party. Later that night, Emilia phoned my house. I had instructed my mother to lie, saying that I had gone to bed because I wasn't feeling well. My mother didn't lie; I think she forgot, but I found it difficult to forgive her for that. Afterwards, Emilia didn't speak to me for a month, and, even though she said later that all was forgiven, things never were the same again. Sometimes I wonder if that's how life is: We make decisions, we make mistakes, and then nothing is ever the same again.

Nevertheless, I didn't think about Emilia again that night, or about anything else besides the party. I knew Earl would be there, because Earl was invited to all the parties. I hadn't gone to many parties then, only the ones organized by the school, which were usually boring because nobody danced and the school gym was cold and too brightly lit.

I convinced my mother to buy me a new dress, promising to wear it again for graduation. We chose one made of light blue velvet, with a full skirt that swirled out when I turned, and a collar and short sleeves trimmed with white lace. With my almost-white blonde hair, I even began to feel pretty. My mother combed my hair in a page-boy and allowed me to use a little of her perfume. When I came down the stairs, my father let out a heart-felt whistle of admiration that made me blush with delight. I spun around a couple of times so he could see the skirt swirl and then, giving him a kiss, got into the car with my mother. She accompanied me to the door of Susan's house, pecked me on the cheek, and said she'd pick me up at eleven.

Suddenly I found myself alone in the entrance hall. The

maid had run back to the kitchen after closing the front door. I didn't dare move even though I could hear music and voices in the living room. On the left, the wall was covered with a giant mirror, and I couldn't avoid seeing myself in it. I felt pretty for the first time in my life; my blonde hair was shiny and it came just below my ears, curling softly inward at the ends. My eyes looked intensely blue matching the color of my dress; excited anticipation had painted my cheeks a soft pink. I smiled. That's how Earl would see me. I was just about to turn away from my image when I saw reflected in the mirror a sudden movement between the greens in the planter behind me. Quickly turning my head, I discovered a tiny kitten crouched under the wide leaves of a fern.

"Oh, how cute! Come here kitty, kitty, kitty!" I said, picking up the little ball of fur and hugging it against my chest. "How pretty! You're so cute. What's your name?" I asked the terrified animal, as it made a vain attempt to escape my embrace by climbing up my shoulder.

At that moment I heard Earl's laughter from the other room and then felt something warm and damp run down my chest. Horrified, I threw the kitten back into the plants. Too late. Now the mirror reflected an image of my dress with a bright yellow stain that oozed down the front of it as far as my waist. I could smell the nauseating stench of diarrhea. I wasn't pretty any more. I was absurd, stupid, stained, dirty, and stinking. I was the ugliest and stupidest girl in the world, and I reeked of cat poop. Tears rolled down my face, adding more stains to the already violated front of the dress. I wanted to die.

Susan's mother found me a short while later huddled in the corner of the bathroom, crying, and she did what she could to restore my dress and my face, but nothing could rescue the image of that pretty girl that I had glimpsed in the mirror just a few minutes earlier, destroyed forever by my fondling of the kitten. She managed to get rid of the excrement and the smell with a lot of water and a little cologne, but the dress had a dark, glaring stain in front and my heart was tight with shame and disappointment.

I entered the living room with my head down, found a chair in a corner, and sat praying that the hours would pass quickly and eleven o'clock would come, along with my mother. I didn't have anybody to talk to or to find refuge with because Emilia, my soulmate, the only one who really understood me, was at home, betrayed and deceived. I didn't remember ever feeling so alone. When I dared to raise my eyes, I saw Earl on the other side of the room, chatting with his usual buddies. He wasn't looking in my direction and that, for the first time, seemed like a blessing. The last thing I wanted was for him to see me. Some kids were dancing as we did back then, two steps to the left, two steps to the right, but most of the guests had formed small groups around the table laden with soda pop and sandwiches, and they laughed and talked in loud voices as if they were having a great time. Since I couldn't even imagine what it would be like to be having a great time, I didn't believe their laughter nor their words and I kept my head down for a long time, sitting in the corner, counting the geometric designs on the Persian rug at my feet. Suddenly a shadow cut off the light that allowed me to distinguish the figures, and a hand appeared, extended toward me as an invitation.

"Want to dance?"

It was Earl. He was standing in front of me, waiting for me to take his hand. There was no escape. Numbly I took his outstretched hand, straightened up, and followed him to the center of the dance floor. I'm sure I wasn't breathing. In my throat there was a dove that furiously beat its wings to get out, and the bottom of my stomach had turned into a whirlpool. I felt Earl slip his arm around my waist and pull me toward him, but I couldn't believe it was really happening. I didn't resist at all; it would have been impossible. I had died and gone to heaven in a fraction of a second, and nothing was left of my own free will.

As I followed the two steps that seemed so awkward when the others danced, I felt I was floating as lightly as a leaf in his arms. I closed my eyes and leaned my head forward until my temple rested against his cheek, and remembered what I imagined that my mother felt when she danced with my father at home, his arm encircling her tiny waist, whirling around and around the dining room to the tunes of a waltz. Everything else faded away as the song "I Only Have Eyes For You" convinced me that the rest of the universe had done me the favor of disappearing: "Are the stars out tonight? I don't know if it's cloudy or bright, 'cause I only have eyes for you, dear," so Earl and I could dance eternally and the sensation that overwhelmed me would never end. A faint smell of Old Spice filled my nostrils, which had stopped breathing normally and only absorbed what came from the body that was rubbing gently against mine, my body of a girl about to become a woman, my body without breasts and with scarcely the beginning of a waist where Earl's arm was holding me.

When the song was over I opened my eyes. Earl let me go but he didn't stop looking at me. He smiled again as he had when he asked me to dance. Immediately, another song started and he opened his arms to receive me once more. I melted against him and lost all sense of the boundaries between his body and mine, my muscles turned into thick, trembling gelatin. Earl pulled me closer. I placed my right hand on his shoulder and he hugged my waist with both arms. And so we danced: I was suspended from his neck like a precious jewel, and he held onto me tightly. I remembered how my mother seemed to float in my father's arms as if she weren't touching the floor with her feet, those delicate feet, so beautiful that my father caressed them every night as they sat on the sofa chatting. I remembered the look of ecstasy in my mother's eyes when she gazed at my father, dancing with him, and the way in which they kissed when he arrived home from the office, and how a very fine thread of saliva remained suspended between their two mouths, and I felt that I was just about to enter that marvelous, dreamlike world.

When the second song was over, there was a pause while Susan searched for another record. Earl and I stayed on the dance floor, his hand holding mine as if to ensure that I wouldn't go away, although I knew that I wasn't going anywhere because even that minimal separation was painful and I only wanted the music to start again so I could feel his body against mine once more. I didn't even remember the cat who had threatened to terminate my night, my dreams, my illusion of being seen by him as the prettiest girl at the party.

"What are you doing this summer?"

His words jostled me out of my reverie. At that moment a new song started. I remember it as if it were playing right now; I remember the tune, the title, a phrase. The words escape me because so much time has passed but I know exactly how I heard it that night so many years ago. Earl embraced me once again, and I put my arms around his neck. With an almost inaudible whisper, I replied, "I suppose we'll go to the shore for a few weeks and the rest of the summer I'll be here. And you?"

He leaned his cheek gently against my face and in a soft voice with no inflection to give it any importance, he pronounced my death sentence: "I'm leaving tomorrow. We're moving back to Alabama because my father was transferred.

This is my last night here. Didn't you know? This is my farewell party."

The song seemed to make fun of me, regaling my ears over and over again with the phrase: " . . .and stars fell on Alabama that night," as Earl and I made the last turns around a dance floor that now seemed like the gallows where all my illusions were to be hung, and I was dying inside even more intensely than when I had the accident with the cat.

I know now that it was just the first of many deaths that I would pass through in life, but then it seemed like the end of all endings, the termination of all dreams, the loss of hope. That was the last dance. Most of the parents had already arrived to pick us up. I couldn't even tell him that I loved him; I couldn't even share my pain with him. I felt that my love was absurd; destiny had played a bad joke on me, and I would never recover.

Now, the only reason I've remembered this first love was because yesterday I went to see Emilia who just had her second baby; when I picked him up, he vomited all over the front of my dress. At that moment the words and the music of "Stars Fell On Alabama" came back to me, and to my friend's surprise, I started singing and dancing around the room, hugging the baby against my soiled chest, with the image of Earl and a thirteen-year-old girl whirling as if in a dreamworld on an innocent, golden night, so long ago.

THE JUDAS-TAIL

Before the effect there is the cause, but sometimes at such a distance in time and space that it's not possible to establish the relationship, and the observer thinks he is contemplating a case of entelechy or the triumph of coincidence and chance over the laws of cause and effect.

This may or may not have anything to do with the following tale, or even with the judas-tail, for that matter; it depends on how you look at it and whether you favor a cyclical or linear interpretation of events. Among those favoring a cyclical interpretation, one would have to distinguish between the endorsers of the spiral version (same point, different level) and those of the circle view (same point, same level). The linearists may choose to continue reading this story or not: It won't make much difference. Spiralists will need a millimetric measure and a huge magnifying glass in order to refute the arguments of the circlists, and I'm afraid that in the long run it will boil down to optimists against pessimists. As far as I'm concerned, I'll tell the tale the way I heard it and leave it at that.

I was part of a team studying the classification of serpents in a certain area of the Mexican countryside. Actually, I was along as an observer and a sometime assistant. This suited my love-hate relationship with snakes because of which I can neither throw myself into their study nor leave them in peace. In the region under investigation there were a lot of snakes of the boa family, incredible creatures around three yards long, brown with yellow diamond-shaped designs on their backs. These unusual reptiles hold a special interest for the scientific community due to the fact that they are viviparous and still have vestiges of primitive legs on both sides of their bodies, as if they had once walked. Of all the snakes, these are the easiest to domesticate and some people use them to catch mice or serve as watch dogs. They aren't poisonous and generally kill their prey by constriction. If bothered, they have been known to strangle a man, but their normal diet consists of small mammals and birds. I recount all this so no one will doubt the tale I am about to tell.

On the final day of the study, we arrived at a small, poor, desolate place called Buenatierra, an absurd name since all around there was nothing but dry earth and dust. "This was a real paradise once," said the old farmer who met me at the entrance of the town. "Those four hills around the valley used to be green all year long; they created a barrier against the wind and frost, so that the first inhabitants could harvest two crops a year."

He pointed to four gray mounds that looked like enormous, wind-worn stones abandoned in the midst of a barren plain due to an esthetic oversight of the gods. As for protection against the wind, just ask my hat.

"The river used to flow right through there" he added, pointing to a dry, dusty ditch, "and on that flat area over there grew the plumpest, most succulent corn in the region."

The rest of the group had gone searching for the serpents while I gleaned important information from the town's inhabitants. The old man seemed quite willing to talk, besides being the only soul I had run into. We were walking slowly toward his plot when I asked him if there were any boa constrictors around the place.

"No, sir. We don't see any of those. But we have a lot of snakes we call judas-tails, sort of long, brown critters with a kind of yellow diamond-shaped drawing on their backs."

He watched me write "judas-tail" under the heading of *Boas.*

"But we don't mess with them. No, sir. Around here, we just leave them be, though I can't say the same for them, so we got to take good care of cows with calves, and nursing mothers, lock 'em up 'til the babes can eat by themselves. The snakes hypnotize them, see, they hypnotize them by rubbing against their arms and breasts, staring into their eyes and dancing back and forth, like this, back and forth, rubbing and rubbing till they're half asleep, the women or the cows, I mean. Then they drink the milk. They stick their judas' tail in the calf's or the baby's mouth like this," and he stuck the tip of his finger between his lips, "and then the snake drinks all the milk, the cow's or the woman's, it's the same thing. And even worse, after that she goes back—the cow or the woman—every day to the same place where the judas-tail sucks the milk until she—the cow or the woman—is all dried up, as dried up and parched as this damn earth or as Dried-up Didi was after her baby died of hunger."

"Dried-up Didi?"

"That's what they called her around here. Her real name was Dolores. I never met her 'cause she'd already left when I arrived, but they were still talking about what had happened so I heard the story. According to those that knew her, the day she left—seems she was always 'about' to leave—the day she left and didn't come back, she was just like a dry leaf floating in the wind, like a fig-shell after the worms have eaten the innards.

She went over that way," and he pointed between two of the dry hills. "Some say she was following the judas-tail, others that she was looking for her dead baby since she was half crazy by then, as if her brain had dried up with the rest of her. Everybody expected her to come back, as she always did, but that time she didn't, and no one ever saw her again. When I got here—I was just a young whippersnapper back then and Buenatierra still lived up to its name!—when I arrived Didi had just been gone three or four days and the guys in the cantina were still talking about her and placing bets on whether or not she'd return. There was those that said yes, and those that said no, but my buddy Pedro, the one who had insisted I come here 'cause the harvests were so good, well he said that a coyote had eaten her for certain and she wasn't ever coming back. The bartender just laughed and said that for sure not even a coyote would be interested in that parched bag of bones, and everyone laughed with him, though God only knows what I was laughing at 'cause I didn't even know her. No one ever made good on those bets, though, because by the time we realized that she wasn't coming back, we had other problems and no one was remembering the matter of Didi, as she was called before they called her Dried-up Didi. By then, everyone was talking about the crops and if they were going to fail that year or not; and they failed, yup, there was no harvest that year and I cursed my buddy Pedro for convincing me to sell everything and move here, but there wasn't a thing I could do at that point. We had frost that year and the next, and the rains just seemed to stop during the rainy season. That was when the river I told you ran through here began to dry up, and rumors had it that it was Didi's fault, because of her and the damned judas-tail, that all the goodness of the place had just plain been sucked out of the earth. After all, she was the first woman to arrive here, she and Juan, her man. Before they arrived, there was nobody here, and she was the one that said to Juan, 'Let's settle here; the corn will grow well.' 'Cause this was still a paradise, all green right to the top of those bald hills, all green. I guess that's why they held Didi responsible, since she was the first to settle here long before the frost and the drought."

As the old man talked, we wandered together a way down the road until stopping under the fragmented shadow of an acacia tree. The old rancher leaned over and pinched a bit of yellow dust. "This is all that's left, this here dust and the wind that just blows and blows ever since the hills dried up," he muttered.

"Dolores and Juan were running away from her father who said that no two-bit Juan was going to take his little girl away, but he did, Juan I mean, and they came here looking for a place to settle and start a farm, because back then they still loved each other, at least that's what Pedro said, even though he didn't know them back then either because he also came from someplace else, but his good friend, Doña Lupe, who died shortly after the first frost, told him about those early days in Buenatierra, and he passed the story on to me just the day after Lupe's funeral, when I had just arrived and everybody was still talking about the strange frost that year and betting on whether or not Didi would return.

"She was one of the prettiest women ever seen around here according to Doña Lupe. She was like made of water: two black eyes like dark pools in a stream, her brown skin so humid that when she walked it seemed like she was swimming, and then the long black hair flowing like a lazy brook down the riverbed of her back. Well, the way Doña Lupe described her was almost too much for the imagination, Pedro used to say. Juan, according to my buddy, never left her alone, just dipping his hands into that beauty as though he couldn't stop caressing her.

"They said it was like submerging your fingers in the damp earth, like finding an underground river. And she adored Juan, there was no doubt about that. When he swore that she was the first and only woman for him, she would answer that he too was the first and only man for her, and Doña Lupe said it gave her a real bad feeling to see so much love spilling over when there was so little in the world.

"But Didi was telling the truth because there never was another, well another man anyway. No, Didi never knew another man. Everybody swore to that. And Juan, well, he didn't have time. . .

"Here's where they must have stood when they arrived, and over there," he pointed to a group of huts huddled together, "they built their little home, the first one in Buenatierra, and it was real nice. Didi always kept everything clean or, at least that's what Pedro said that Doña Lupe told him, 'It was the cleanest and prettiest hut in the place,' Lupe had explained, because it wasn't very long before others came and settled nearby. Word spread of the abundance here, who knows how, and people began to arrive and they built their huts and planted their crops and before you knew it, this here was a village. In six months, no more according to Doña Lupe, there was a cantina and that, she said—although I don't agree—was Buenatierra's downfall. She said that work was so easy around here because of the fertility and everything, that the men just put the seeds in the ground and they were assured of a good harvest, and then off they went to spend all their time in the cantina. That's why she said the cantina was the town's downfall, but who knows? I don't think a man's bad just 'cause he wets his whistle now and then, as long as he does his duty and doesn't harm anyone, but that was Doña Lupe's opinion.

"Pedro didn't agree with her either; as a matter of fact, we were in the cantina when he told me all this, and what harm could we do that the frost hadn't already done? But, I'm telling you the way he told it to me and how Doña Lupe had told it to him. So, as I was saying, several months after Didi and Juan settled here, Buenatierra already had an enclosure for drunks and troublemakers so they wouldn't hurt themselves or anybody else, so you could rightly call it a town."

The wind had died down a bit and the shade of the acacia had reached the stone it had been pursuing since midday. We sidled over to the shade and sat down. Now and then I'd whisk away an ant that threatened to crawl up my leg. The old man kept on talking. According to what he had heard, Juan didn't go to the cantina, at least not at first. He said that Didi was like a spring of fresh water and why would he want anything else to drink. Besides, she was pregnant although nothing showed for a long time and Juan took to caring for her.

"She must have been six or seven months along. . . yes, that must be right because that is when Pedro came to town and that would be why he never saw how beautiful she was. He told me that Doña Lupe talked of nothing else but how Didi was going to pot and what a shame, such a pretty girl. Because, by the time Pedro got here she had lost her nymph-like figure: First her breasts became so swollen that she was hunched over by their weight; then her belly swelled up, which was natural, but hers was twice the normal size. And it wasn't just her belly: She was swollen all the way around. Pedro said you couldn't tell if she was coming or going unless you looked at her face. And this awful swelling spread from her middle upwards. Her face was like a balloon," and he made a circle with his hands on either side of his head, "her eyes, which had been like pools, were no more than piss-holes in the snow. Then she got pimples all over her forehead and chin, and because they were so big and her skin was so dark, they looked like bruises, as if someone had beaten her. But Pedro swore that Juan never hit her, although he probably wanted to, according to my buddy. Pedro did get to know Juan, although they were never good friends because by then Juan spent all his time in the cantina, drunk and crying, 'Oh, my sweet Didi,' 'I've lost my Didi,' 'My Didi is gone forever,' as if his wife weren't one and the same woman he had married. But, then she didn't look the same because all that swelling had destroyed everything lovely about her. She didn't even comb her hair anymore, according to Doña Lupe, because her breasts were so large they kept her from lifting her arms. Her locks were dull and tangled; they looked more like tumble-weed blowing in the wind than the dark stream they had once been. She apparently didn't wash her clothes either or even bathe herself because she couldn't crouch down on the river-bank anymore or bend over in the water. People began to say she stank and that being near her was like being in the cantina when the drunks started puking. Maybe that's why Juan began going there; he must have thought that it was the same thing, smelling the drunks and smelling his wife, and soon he couldn't smell anything anyway because he was drunk and puking too, and then he would go on and on about how Didi used to be. Pedro says that that's how he found out the truth in everything Doña Lupe told him."

The old man was quiet for a moment, gazing at what was left of the "town," as he called it. His hut was the farthest away from the center group because he had been the last to arrive. Word had gotten out, he said, that Buenatierra was ruined after the first frost and people stopped coming, they started going elsewhere or stayed on their own plots, however barren they might have been. It was getting late; the shade of the acacia had covered the stone and passed on. Soon, the others of my group would be back.

"But you asked me about the judas-tail. Don't think I'd forgotten; I was getting there, because it was just when Juan was in the cantina and Didi was so pregnant that the damned traitor showed up. Yes, damned, because if you want to know what I believe, well it's that the snake ruined this town and nothing else. Yup, all because of the damned judas-tail snake. 'Cause it wasn't Juan's fault that his wife got so ugly it drove him to drink in order to be able to remember her as she was; and, how can the cantina be blamed, if a cantina is just there and doesn't make anyone drink? And Pedro can't tell me that Doña Lupe didn't stand at the door asking him to buy her a beer. So you can't say it was the cantina's fault. And even Dolores, who can lay the blame on her? How could she know she was going to get so ugly with the baby that not even her husband wanted to see her? Poor Dolores, what did she even know about snakes if there were none where she came from, so she probably wasn't even afraid of them, or at least not like the women around here are now. Actually, the folks in these parts didn't worry about snakes because they didn't come into the valley; there were snakes in the dry lands on the other side of the hills, but they didn't come around here, not until that judas-tail showed up. And ever since then, there are a whole lot of judas-tails in these parts, no other kind of snake, just judas-tails. That's why those of us who still have cows take care of them so they aren't sucked dry and their calves don't die of hunger. And those who still have young wives are extra careful; they guard them even more than the cows. Even though they say that what happened to Dolores won't happen again in a thousand years, they sure bolt their doors carefully when their wives are breastfeeding, so they can't fool me."

It seemed to bother him that young people didn't believe the story. He frowned and mumbled again, "They can't fool me."

I thought he had finished and wasn't going to say any more. I began to feel impatient watching him staring off into the distance as if there were nothing else to look at, as if the distance were the only reality, so I prompted him, "And Dolores, what happened to her?"

He shook off his lethargy and gave me a sad look.

"Poor Didi," he said, as if he had known her. "She probably felt really lonely when Juan started going to the cantina, because they had been like this," and he crossed his fingers to show how close they were, "so she never had to make friends with the other townsfolk. They were always together, Juan and Didi, up until then. But, when Juan wasn't with her all day, when he never set foot in their hut except to yell at her, then all she did was cry. Juan would come home drunk and holler, 'You took my Didi away from me; you've got your baby now, so you don't need me; you just let yourself go to pot and now I don't want you any more!' And Didi would cry, not just when he yelled at her, but all day long, by herself because she didn't have anybody to visit her, no friends. And crying she'd get even uglier, 'cause when a woman cries her eyes swell all up and they look terrible, and Didi's eyes were already swollen before that. So she'd cry, and she'd pop those purple pimples, and she'd talk to herself, and who knows what she'd talk about 'cause everything she knew came from Juan. At least, she talked to herself until the judas-tail showed up. That was just a bit before the baby was born.

"Lupe said, and who knows how she knew, but Pedro said she found out everything that went on in Buenatierra, so it must be true. Anyway, Lupe said that one day she was walking by Dolores' hut and she heard her say, 'You're a lonely critter, too, aren't you?' And Lupe wondered who the hell she was talking to, seeing as she didn't have any friends, so she peeked through the open door and saw Didi sitting on her straw mat talking and talking to this big snake, and the snake seemed to be listening to her. He'd raise his head to the level of hers, and rock his body back and forth," the old man rocked back and forth as he talked, "then, Didi said, 'I'm so lonely! I miss my Juan!' and the tears rolled down her swollen cheeks and the snake just rocked back and forth 'til she stopped crying.

"When Pedro told me this story, I thought it was pretty strange, talking to a snake and all that, but he said that Lupe didn't think much of it since it was like Didi was talking to herself, so after a while she forgot about it and didn't say anything. But that doesn't fool me; that Lupe was crafty, and later, when the whole story came out, she was the one who said the snake should be called a 'judas-tail' for the way he'd betrayed someone who gave him so much warmth, so she didn't forget it that much.

"All this was right before the baby was born, Didi's of course because Doña Lupe never had any children; she never married, said it was more peaceful that way, alone and without problems, Doña Lupe I mean, because Dolores wasn't used to being alone, and when Juan left her for so long, she probably suffered a lot. I suppose that's the only explanation for what happened with the snake.

"I guess when Juan left early in the morning and wasn't fixin' to come back 'til late, that critter would show up and Didi would talk to him, pouring her heart out, poor thing, crying like she did all the time. And while she was talking, the snake would sway back and forth like I told you before, and the swaying would hypnotize her until she fell into a trance. Then she'd stop crying and fall asleep and not wake up until Juan came back shouting at the top of this voice. By then the judas-tail had disappeared, so Juan didn't find out about the snake until it was too late.

"On the day she gave birth, Pedro was in the cantina and

Juan was there as usual. Pedro says that Juan was on his seventh drink and Pedro knew this because they used to count Juan's drinks to see on which one he'd get drunk and start crying. Sometimes it was the sixth and sometimes it was the seventh. Well, that day he was on the seventh and he still wasn't crying, when Lupe ran up shouting that Didi had given birth. As Lupe told it, she was passing by the hut when she heard a baby crying and she knew that Dolores had had the baby. My guess is that Lupe was spying on her, but Pedro says no, that Lupe respected other people's privacy, but I'm thinking how else did she find out about everything?

"When Juan heard Lupe's yelling, he raced home, probably thinking that his Didi without the baby would be like she was before. But, no sir, she wasn't. Didi without the baby was just like Didi with the baby, except maybe her roundness was a little flabbier, so Juan went back to the cantina. That's what Pedro told me, because he was there when Juan got back and he says barely twenty minutes had gone by, scarcely time for him to get home, take a look and come back.

"Poor little kid. His father didn't love him because he had destroyed his mother's beauty, and I suppose Dolores didn't love him for the same reason, or maybe it was on account of the judas-tail who kept visiting her every day even after the baby was born. Apparently, while the tyke nursed, Didi talked to the snake, and the snake would sway back and forth until she fell asleep and then, according to Lupe, it would climb up on her and stick the end of its tail in the baby's mouth and suckle the milk that should have been for the little one, and that old judas-tail would rub itself and rub itself back and forth between the mother's breasts. Of course, the baby got thinner and thinner, until his poor little eyes were sunken into their sockets when they had been so bright and wide-open since the first day he was born: a sure sign he was going to be a bright little tot. Lupe said she was afraid from the start that the baby was going to die but that it wasn't her place to butt into other's affairs. She wasn't a 'buttinski' she said, so she kept still. That's what Pedro told me and the way I see it although I didn't say anything to him 'cause Lupe was a real close friend and she had just passed away and it's not healthy to badmouth the dead, but the way I see it, if Lupe had spoken up sooner nothing would have happened and Dolores would be here taking care of her grandchildren and this valley would still be the paradise it once was. But who knows? Blaming Didi for the frost doesn't make much sense; one thing's the weather and another a woman. They're two different things. My guess is the harvest would have been lost anyway. But, like I was saying, Doña Lupe didn't say anything until it was too late. Pedro said that she was passing by Didi's house one afternoon on the way to her hut and she didn't hear the baby crying as she usually did, so she stuck her nose in the door to see what was happening. Well, the way Pedro tells it makes your hair stand on end. He says that Lupe saw Dolores lying on the straw mat, but this time (And that's why I think Lupe spied on her, 'cause why else would she have called it 'this time?'), well, this time Dolores wasn't asleep. Her eyes were rolled back 'til the whites showed and she was trembling all over, not from the cold 'cause it wasn't cold that day, but because that damn judas-tail was rubbing against her legs and belly and between her breasts. And the tip of his tail wasn't in the baby's mouth because by then the baby was unconscious, with his eyes closed, white as a ghost, and my guess is that he was already dead, so the tip of the judas-tail's tail (sounds funny, doesn't it? the judas-tail's tail) was between Dolores' legs and she was shaking like she was going to die, with her eyes all rolled back and her fingernails clawing the earthen floor as if she were plowing a field. Pedro says that's when Lupe realized that she should tell somebody 'cause if not the baby was going to die, though he probably was already dead. Lupe ran to the cantina and told Juan, and that day nobody knew how many drinks he had bucketed down, but he was drunk for sure because he couldn't get the snake off from around his neck. What the hell; if you're going to die, its better to die drunk so you don't really know what's happening. Pedro says that Lupe didn't want to go back to Dolores' hut to see what was going on, so he figured he had better run and see if Juan needed help, even though they were just drinking buddies. But, by the time Pedro got there, he couldn't help Juan or the baby. They were both dead, the baby had starved to death and Juan had been strangled, his eyes all bulging out and his face purple. That was all he found: There was no murdering judas-tail and no Didi, though she did come back the day of the funeral.

"That day, when they saw her, Pedro says, everyone was convinced that Lupe had told the truth, because seeing Dolores all skin and bones, with only a couple of pounds of sagging flesh on her, all dried up as if somebody or something had been sucking the life out of her, well, nobody doubted Lupe's story anymore. That was when they started calling her Dried-up Didi, but they didn't say it to her face because nobody spoke to her ever again.

"For a while, there was talk of banishing her from Buenatierra, since even though she went out into the hills every morning, and who knows why unless it was as Lupe said, looking for the judas-tail, and that's possible because every time she came back she was even more dried up, but she still came back every night to sleep with the ghosts of her two men, her husband and her baby. But while they were trying to decide whether or not to banish her, she went and disappeared and then I arrived here, like I told you. Now that I think of it, I showed up the day they were burying Lupe. The day before Lupe hadn't shown up at the door of the cantina and some neighbors went looking for her. Well, they found her lying dead on her cot, as if she had passed away in her sleep, with a strange, almost malicious smile on her face. The way Pedro tells it, her expression was so spooky they hurried the funeral in order to put her safely underground as fast as possible.

"By then, Dolores had disappeared, and as I told you at the beginning, they were still placing bets on whether or not she'd come back, and she never did.

"But you were asking me about snakes, and I ended up telling you this long tale that can't possibly interest you. How a body talks when there's nothing else to do! No matter how much you till this earth, it doesn't produce anything anymore. The same thing happened the other day; a stranger passed through here and who knows what he asked me but I ended up telling him the whole story. And when I finished, he just laughed and said some weird thing about apples. I'm telling you! But if you're looking for snakes, the only ones you'll find around here are judas-tails. That's why we keep close watch over the few cows that have calves, and we guard our women when we have them, even more. Like I said from the start: It's better not to mess with those judas-tails, yes sir, much better."

THE TURTLE

Near the beach the sea becomes transparent. A radiant sun extends its blanket of light over the water; the brilliance shatters and sails on sparkles of random swells. From the depths, blue-green lances of light pierce the waves, spread, and are lost on the surface. The air grows still and rests, and the gentle breathing of the sea repeats "ussh, ahhhh" across the long tongue of white beach, depositing a battered coconut on the sand. Myriad fish sketch a translucent geometry with reflections from their fins. In its depth, far from the shore the sea reverberates and sings.

In secret fibers of an ancestral memory, the sea turtle registers the glowing, fervid vibrations, feels their resonance in her ample body, and follows her dark impulse. She breathes and dives, breaking the mirror of water with her hard shell, leaving behind a wake of bubbles, and then emerges. She is near. In the folds of her strong neck, in the softness of her belly, she absorbs messages from disparate layers of the sea, some warm, some cool. She approaches the beach, all trembling and joy, scattering gleams and sparkles across the surface. She is near; she is returning. In her own flesh, engraved in the darkness, she finds the memory of that other primal darkness, and something inside her sings. Bird of the water, kite of the deep sea, she returns with the tug of a tenacious string, and true to instinct, follows just one command: nest.

The man hurries toward the beach, sliding down the side of the dune. He stops, feels the sun at its zenith, shades his eyes with a hand, his glance fans across the sea. The reflection blinds him momentarily, his pupils adjust to the brilliance, and then he spots them: small dark mounds floating on the silky luster of the water. He spins on his heels, strides rapidly up the dune, instinctively following his own footprints, and disappears. The day's splendor quickly closes over the wound of his presence.

The limitless solitude of water shines, an extensive and beautiful loneliness. The sea. The breeze and its tributaries make paths of light, weaving an agile tapestry of sun. The turtle hovers in strange expectation, floating tranquilly without knowing, without asking, feeling the cycle that is approaching in the fullness of her belly. She is possessed by powerful energy, the same energy that compelled her to break the eggshell and emerge, so tiny that her initial race down the beach to the sea seemed unending, dodging dangers, mountains and valleys of sand, the claw of a crab, until she was picked up by the edge of a wave, tumbled about, dragged into the water, and sent on her prolonged journey. And now she returns, treading on the almost-forgotten echoes of that beginning and feeling once again the urgency of life, suddenly recognizing her own yearning in another turtle that is swimming nearby.

In the shelter of the bay the boats rock quietly on gentle, lapping waves. The man arrives and whistles, another hurries to meet him. They speak and their gestures disturb the stillness. They look at the sun, make calculations, nod in agreement, and walk away.

The beach is calm at midday. A wafting breeze pushes at the tide, combs the palm trees, and retreats. The sun dominates the landscape; its sparkles collide and reflect each other as they break into bits of color among the grains of sand. The water brushes lazily over the sand, leaving lacy patterns on the beach. Suddenly a wave swells and crashes, tumbling into foam and spray, then withdraws. The turtle waits no longer; her nostrils are full of a scent that awakens and paralyzes her. Her companion silently begins a strange aquatic dance, rubbing her shell with his flippers, bumping her gently with his head, in a mute sequence of signals. The dance, the signals, the soft shoves all make her restless, but they also quell her impulse to escape. She is all instinct and need, an ancestral memory that dictates her responses and subdues her fear. Inside she carries a treasureload of large, mature eggs, still dormant but eager for life.

A hungry dog emerges from the bushes, sniffs the air, and stands still. Across the burning sand the seagulls embroider their intricate discourse. A crab scurries for his life. The dog moves, her drooping teats swing back and forth as she trots across the sand. The gulls fly up with a squawking protest, circle once, then land a short distance away. The dog looks at them; hunger festers in her belly and waits.

In the water, the couple is not in a hurry. The striking sunlight that makes them open and close their eyes, the heat of the midday, and the warmth of the surface-water lull their movements to a slow sway, a gradual approach. She is still, he swims around her, watching her lethargy settle in. Then, a strange movement and she feels the jawbone of the male on her back. Her flippers come alive, but he has already mounted, holding her still with his strong claws. A hefty revolving of shells stirs up the surrounding water, putting an end to the calm. The female feels the weight of the male, his harsh claws grasping her back, and she tries to free herself. She struggles to flee to the tranquility of deep water when suddenly she is overwhelmed by the unexpected rupture of her solitude and the imminence of a strange plenitude in which the limits of her own existence are dissolved. Something is completed, something fulfilled and perfected that connects all the facets of her wandering and binds them together in silence. The restlessness of her secret eggs seems to swell almost to the point of bursting. Gently the coupling turtles are rocked by the ample embrace of the sea.

The breeze diminishes. The great silk-cotton tree extends its blanket of heavy shade over the hut. The heat dozes outside. The dog appears at the door, growls at the puppy that approaches her, and enters furtively, a shadow among shadows, close to the wall. She lies down on the cool floor, her snout trembling against the hard earth: Two cautious eyes observe. The man at the table clanks his spoon against the metal plate, sips the watery soup, stirs and sips, his head down, his eyes fixed. A transistor radio fills the air with static; a woman's voice sings; the static returns. The child cries. Crouching before the fire the woman heats up tortillas. "Shhh, shhh." Handing the tortillas to the man, she stands and picks up her child, "shhh, shhh." From the folds of her blouse she pulls a swollen breast, the little mouth catches it, the woman crouches down again next to the fire. In the shadow lies the dog; only her eyes move, from the woman to the child to the man to the woman. The man noisily pushes his plate away from him, the dog starts and jumps up. "Get out!" He throws a beer bottle after her retreating tail. The bottle rolls and stops next to a stone, pierced by a sharp ray of sunshine.

Gradually the sun surrenders its reign. The afternoon breeze pushes rows of white clouds, stirs them up, and forms them again. Over the mountain the pallid pupil of the moon appears, contemplates the landscape for a moment, then blacks out behind a cloud. The female turtle is slowly pulled into the dance, shell on top of shell, she tilts and rocks to the rhythm of the water. Over and over again they separate and seek each other, they dive and surface, oblivious to time. A pelican glides through the air, swoops down, dives into the water, emerges, shakes himself, and swallows, once more takes off with a heavy flapping of wings. The turtle is lost in an ageless memory that has the voice of the sea and the colors of the air, the coming and going of millions of years, the plenitude of closed cycles. Her flesh sings, rejoices, and opens to the registry of storms and calm, vital, vibrant, full of the rhythm of tides. The sky takes on purple and salmon tones, orange, and a tenuous yellow. Across the sea there are paths of color, early shadows tremble with uncertainty, over the mountain a cautious moon dares to show itself.

The cradle rocks to the rhythm of a distracted hand. With a different rhythm, the other hand combs limp hair, reviving its shine in the light of the fire. The man sits up in the hammock, puts his feet on the floor, takes a knife and stone from the wall. He hones, sharpens, prepares. "I want to get there early." The woman gets up, the cradle settles; she picks up a bag and prepares a taco with beans and a tortilla. The man snaps his fingers, the dog comes running, and together they start down the path.

The blind eye of the moon opens onto the sea; waves crash in crystals of light, drawing ephemeral crisscross patterns. The turtle's strange urgency is reborn inside her; the water feels hostile; her desire changes and she rejects the male. Her body is tense with longing for the beach, a pressing need for land. Her flippers propell her toward the swell of the waves, the thundering sound of the reef. The weight of her body rises and is thrust forward with the swirling water; the memory buried in her flesh travels in reverse, out of the water, upwards to the beach. An accommodating wave deposits her on the sand. She begins to row laboriously with her flippers, but her shell and flesh are heavy, and the answer to her urgency is awkward and slow.

Against the moon appears the silhouette of the man, and with him, the hungry dog. His hand calms the animal; his eyes have seen something. It looks like a trunk or driftwood, but it moves, slowly. "Stay!" He kneels in the sand; the dog slumps down.

Along paths of moonlight the turtle progresses with a cumbersome crawl that occupies her whole being, totally committed to leaving behind her natural medium. She is unusually inept away from the smooth gliding of water, as she pushes upward toward the highest part of the beach. Behind her she leaves a wide, symmetric trail with her fins: hard, determined paddles that strain forward, pulling along her heavy bulk. She stops, breathes with difficulty, snorts. She starts again, conquering the beach little by little, recognizing her origin in a wordless memory, and hearing the strong echoes of the beginning: nest.

Eyes watch her from the dune; dog and master lie on the sand, waiting. The turtle is slow. Another shadow approaches and crouches down. The man growls, "I saw her first. She's mine." The shadow straightens up and moves away. In the man's memory, the hut and the child sleep, the woman keeps watch.

Fatigue seems to have stopped the turtle completely. She rises up on her flippers, lets out a deep sigh, and continues. An obscure, profound recognition of the sand vibrates in her flesh. Something alerts her and she swirls the sand around her, making the first bed. She rests and begins dragging her weight forward again. It wasn't the place. A new sign and the flippers round out a space. Once again she doesn't finish. The secret memory searches and reminisces.

The dog whines softly; the man glances at the moon. He counts the beds. Five. "Damn!" He looks at the moon again and gets restless. The shadow of the other man reappears. In his hand, a bag full of eggs. He gives a little laugh. "That one's yours," he says.

"Fuck you!" is the answer.

⊡

She is totally focused on the discovery; she dives into the new bed and knows. She feels hurried now, her flippers like sharp shovels gauge out the hole, a perfect cylinder. The sand flies. The turtle's insides are exploding. Something in her is complete, filling her with ownership. She's there now, fulfilled, and her whole existence surrenders to the rhythm of nature.

⊡

The man eagerly crawls across the sand, approaching cautiously, spying on the process. The dog behind him sniffs, her nostrils filled with the smell of eggs. The man contemplates the shiny, white spheres, reflections of the moon, balls of light that fall slowly into the shadows. The turtle, absorbed in her own consummation, doesn't perceive them. For her the perfect space is open, the cylinder of the nest, and from the center of her being she slowly closes the cycle.

The man counts, his eyes fixed on the nest that is being filled. But the turtle stops to rest, with many more eggs still inside her. She lays her hard jawbone on the sand, and once more her flesh rejoices and sings.

The dog becomes impatient and barks. The turtle awakens from her trance. Startled, she shakes herself. Her flesh closes, her flippers push at the sand, covering, hiding, protecting the nest. The cycle has been interrupted.

With his fist the man knocks the dog aside; he grabs the shell of the turtle and turns her over. The blade of the knife flashes in the light of the moon.

Near the highway the men wait, crouching in the shadows. A car approaches, stops, the trunk opens like a giant mouth. The men come forward, they bargain, weaving intricate accounts in the night air. The bags full of eggs are relinquished; extended hands close and return to their pockets.

In the hut the woman keeps watch. She stirs the fire, then stands at the door; the man returns. She backs up against the wall silently. He enters, throws the coins on the table. "Son of a bitch! He cheated me!" And he lies down. In the light of the fire the woman sadly counts, fingering the coins over and over again, then puts them away.

The beach wakes up slowly. The water stretches out sleepily, laps at the sand, and rests. The eye of the sun opens and illuminates the entrails of the dead turtle with eerie tones of red. Across the silky surface of the sea dark mounds appear, here and there. Up on the dune, the silhouette of a man severs the sun in two.

GIFT OF THE JAGUAR

That the jaguar is my nagual,* I have no doubt. He's mine, of that I'm sure because he appeared when I wasn't looking for him and has accompanied me since for better or worse, leaning, perhaps, toward worse. But I have to admit that I haven't always known what's good for me, and many times things that seem bad end up being beneficial, so the jaguar is my nagual, and be it for good or bad, only he would know.

It all started one afternoon when my husband and I were on our way back from having lunch in Querétaro. I had downed a few tequilas and a few beers and whenever I had a few drinks I also smoked a few cigarettes and many times when I did that I had a fight with my husband, and that made me forget everything else like visiting the ladies' room before starting out on the highway. So on the way back I had an irrepressible urge to pee and even though my husband was angry, I insisted.

"Look over there," I said, pointing to a huge building on the side of the road with a sign that said "Antiques & Collectibles."

**Nagual:* animal spirit that guides and protects one in life.

My husband didn't answer, since he wasn't speaking to me after our fight, but he pulled over. I walked carefully, mincing my steps, trying not to leak, and in the bathroom I let loose a river of relief. Upon coming out, I saw that I had entered an enormous warehouse full of antiques, knick-knacks, and diverse objects retrieved from aging estates. Through a side window I saw that my husband wasn't in the car. Scarcely glancing at the merchandise, I quickly crossed the room and went out to the patio to look for him. There they had deposited everything collected in the ruins of haciendas and the patios of families impoverished by the eternal economic crisis: iron gratings; two-legged chairs; tables corroded by use, time, and humidity; doors without frames; and broken-down gates were heaped chaotically here and there. There was no sign of my husband, but there was my nagual, peeking his nose out from under a door that was leaning against his back. The jaguar's dusty face looked at me as if he had been expecting me or had journeyed there to find me. Suddenly the tequila and beer lost their grip; I forgot about my husband's customary grumpy silence and smiled without knowing why. The jaguar-spirit locked in that strange object—whatever it was—needed to be with me; we belonged to each other.

When I managed to get the door off his back, my nagual turned out to be a giant bellows, probably used in the forge of some mine. The orifice that expelled the air was the mouth of the jaguar's head, beautifully sculpted in wood. The jaguar's back was also elegantly engraved and decorated with bronze nails, a style which indicated its origin in the late eighteenth or early nineteenth century. My husband's grumbling, the significant price, and the thousand pounds of weight on our car's shock absorbers were not enough to separate me from the nagual, which I immediately recognized as mine. For the first time in who knows how many years, I imposed my will on anyone who dared to contradict me and, with help from three employees, we lifted the heavy animal onto the back seat of the car as my husband complained bitterly about drunken women and castrating wives and mumbled other insults aimed at the target of my self-esteem.

At home I cleaned, polished, oiled, and burnished the jaguar-bellows with my own hands, putting my heart and soul into it. Nobody understood my passion, but oddly enough they left me alone to do my will. The nagual responded by displaying a mysterious semi-smile and a strange beauty, both spiritual and violent, that only I could appreciate. Although I didn't understand it then, now I know that he had come to change my life and, from that moment on, nothing remained the same.

When the jaguar appeared, I was entering a period of life when I thought that everything was over. My grown children ignored me; my bored husband ignored me; and I, between drinking and smoking, also ignored myself. At fifty-two, I was getting ready to die, doing the same things that I had done for thirty-one years of marriage: cooking, cleaning, arranging things, taking a class to pass the time, eating with friends, going to the hairdresser, lecturing the kids, waiting up for my daughter when she went out at night. In other words, doing what every housewife does every day of her life, and all in the company of my two best friends: alcohol and tobacco.

My nagual went to work immediately. First he took away my children, since both were married in less than a year; then he took away my friend, alcohol, with which I had warmed my soul for so many years so as not to feel life's aggressions. Down the same road as alcohol my cigarettes disappeared, taking with them the smoke that had wrapped around the anger and resentment I was never able to express; I was left with empty hands and a mouth full of reproaches that I hurled at my husband.

Then the nagual took him away, too, or should I say he was taken away by the redhead who called herself my friend and who shared with him the last bottle of whiskey he drank in my house before calling the movers and taking away all of the furniture except the bed and the nagual, since they were mine. The house was in my husband's name and, as soon as it was empty, I realized how much it burdened me and I exchanged it for a little money that the nagual was kind enough not to take away from me.

With that money I set myself up in a small condominium that seemed just my size, over in the southern part of the city, where the sun shines warmer. There I installed my nagual right in the middle of the living room, where a ray of morning sun reaches him through the window that looks out on the volcano Popocateptl. I found a job that I like; I have a suitor or two to treat me well; I spend hours by myself and with my beloved books. I feel happy.

And thus my existence revolves around my jaguar, because when he took everything away, I discovered the gift that he offered me instead: In the spacious freedom of not having anything, I found myself. . . .

THE PROVOCATION

I couldn't stand it any longer. I was observing her from my window for a long time, thinking they should forbid such provocation. She was alone on the grassy divider of the boulevard and she seemed to be waiting for someone or something. I tried to distract myself with work, creating imaginary deadlines. Feeling her presence behind my back shattered my concentration.

I struggled against the dark desire to go down to the street, remembering oaths and promises I had made after my last attack of guilt. Never again! I buried my head in a book. The letters danced on the page. I read one line five times. I looked out the window again. She was still there, caressed by a slight breeze. A man crossed the street, looked at her with longing, and continued on his way. I could breathe again. I controlled my crazy impulse to possess her and started reading out loud to overcome the wave of palpitations that was enveloping me. I heard the noise of a car on the street; it stopped a moment beneath my window and then started up again. I was gripped by the fear of loss; anxiety throbbed in my chest. I swung around and felt a wave of relief when I saw her lush presence outlined by the golden rays of the late afternoon sun. Realizing the inevitability of desire, I postponed my surrender to destiny in order to savor the certainty of possession for a while.

A whiff of perfume invaded my imagination, blinding me to oaths taken in the cold shame of dawn. I envisioned how she would open slowly for me, revealing unexpected depths to her secret yearning. I couldn't hold back any longer. I rushed down the stairs, stopping only to pick up a knife (in case she resisted) and then ran out to the street. I crossed to the divider with feigned indifference; I waited to be sure I wasn't being observed and then I approached her with determination, grabbed her with my hand and took out my knife. She turned toward me willingly, the sharp edge of the blade did its job as she collapsed, raining petals around the sign that implored, "Please don't cut the roses."

WHEN I WAS A HORSE

I was in second grade, so I was past the ordeal of the first year, when we spent the whole time scared to death because the big kids—those already in second grade or above—tortured us first-graders when the teachers weren't watching. Several times they stole my sandwich or a cupcake that my mother had put in my lunch box.

It was mainly the boys, even the ones from our own classroom, who tortured the girls. They in turn were tortured by the big kids, and they took it out on us whenever possible. They almost yanked my braids off and chased me around to lift up my skirt and see my underpants, until I started wearing shorts underneath my uniform. That solved the skirt-lifting problem: I didn't have to run away anymore; I'd just make a face and taunt "naa-na-na-naa-na" when they raised my skirt and saw only shorts.

But in second grade we were bigger; the boys picked on the younger kids who had just started school because they were easy prey, and we girls, who didn't get so much pleasure out of torturing others, spent most of our time forming cliques. If a girl who hadn't been around when we were forming the group wanted to get in, we closed ranks and pretended to be *very important* and we didn't accept her. That was the rule. Speaking to the rejected girl meant exclusion, too, so most of the time the group was reduced to just two girls or it dissolved completely, and we had to form another one that admitted the rejects.

My group included Wendy, Carlotta, Susan, and Paula. The five of us felt like sisters because we had a lot in common, and we were very different from girls in other groups, like the one that brought dolls and played house, or another that made figures out of clay or playdough. One group just sat in a circle and ate; they were so into their food that they hardly even talked. So one day I snuck up close to see what they were eating, but when they saw me they all stopped immediately, covered their lunch boxes, and made faces at me, so I left. I guess their moms had put special food in their boxes, not just peanut butter or tuna sandwiches like mine. As one of the girls in that group was a bit chubby, we teased them, saying they were all going to look like her. But they never kicked her out; I think her mom gave her the best food and that's why they kept her in the group. I guess in some ways, we were as bad as the boys.

But Wendy, Carlotta, Susan, Paula, and I had the best group: We were horses. It never occurred to us to be stallions or mares, since sex meant nothing in a world where you could just be a horse. And during our free time we would gallop across the schoolyard as if it were an endless prairie, neighing, rearing up on our back legs and pawing the air, feeling the wind in our manes, and grazing on what was in our lunch boxes. All during recess we could be seen haughty and proud, like thoroughbreds: self-assured, free, and beautiful. Even today I can remember what it felt like to be a horse, flicking my grand head, shaking my mane, and frolicking along the edge of the yard, reigning over fields, imaginary mountains, and valleys. One neigh and the others came running; then we snorted and rubbed our necks one against the other and we exchanged horse kisses as I had observed the neighbor's horses do.

At first, the boys—Alfred, Joe, Peter, Richard and John—laughed and made fun of us. They were probably envious because they didn't dare romp and gallop and let their manes loose as we did. We paid no attention to them, continuing with our games, enjoying the freedom of not being boys or girls, but just plain "horses." One day Peter, the leader of the boys that were watching and making fun of us, came over to me.

"Hey, what if we were cowboys and pretended to capture all of you," he said.

"Well, okay, but afterwards we'd get away."

"We could pretend that we were branding you. . ."

"You try that, and I'll kick you right in the shins."

After some hemming and hawing, we managed to reach an agreement: We'd be the wild horses and they'd be the cowboys who would try to lasso and tame us. It was a lot of fun for a while. If they managed to catch one of us, they would take her to a section of the yard surrounded by a short picket fence. That was the corral and the captured horse couldn't get out until another of us horses snuck up and saved her by kicking down the fence. I remember feeling an intense emotion while being pursued and captured, and sometimes my underpants got a bit wet from the excitement. I liked it when John chased me because he was the cutest, and sometimes I wouldn't run as fast as I could when he was chasing me: I'd let myself get caught just to feel his hand on my back as he led me to the corral. But once there, I almost never waited to be rescued. Instead, I would rear up on my hind feet and knock down any barrier that they put up, just to show them how brave and strong I was.

"That's cheating! You said you had to wait until another horse rescued you," my captor protested.

"Yup, but not me: I don't need to be rescued. I'm the strongest and bravest and most beautiful horse of all. That's why I'm the leader; that's why I can't be caught, and you can only capture me if I let you."

"Then I can escape, too," Paula protested.

"No, because you're not the leader. And if you escape without our rescuing you, we'll drop you from the group."

This game lasted almost all spring and as a horse, I was unbelievably happy. Recess was the best time of day. Even before class ended, I began to enjoy the excitement I would feel as I raced out into the yard and became a horse, a sensation that lasted until the moment the bell rang calling us back to class.

One day my four horse-friends stopped me before going out to the yard.

"Today you can't escape by yourself, okay?"

"Why not? I always have."

"But not today, or we won't play."

"Okay, but only for today."

Determined not to let myself get trapped, I went out into the yard where the cowboys were waiting for us. I had given my word and if I got caught I would have to stay in the corral until I was rescued by one of my band. I—the fastest, strongest and bravest horse of all—would be humiliated. The best thing to do was not let myself get caught, even when John was after me.

That day I managed to avoid all attempts to capture me. Wendy, Carlotta, Susan, and Paula were all stuck in the corral and I was looping around, trying to figure out how to get to them without being captured, when the bell rang. Assuming the game was over, I stopped running and turned to go back to class, when four of the cowboys caught up with me and grabbed my arms from behind.

"Not fair! The bell rang and you can't catch me anymore," I shouted, trying to free my arms.

They threw me on the ground and, while holding me down, pulled my skirt up over my face. I struggled desperately, but with all four of them restraining me, I couldn't get loose. Then I felt a pair of hands yanking my shorts and underpants down to my knees. I could hear jeers and shouts of glee and triumph, as I tried in vain to kick, bite, or scratch my tormenters. I was filled with deep shame and the desperate need to disappear, or die. Finally they let go of me, and, covering my face with my hands, I rolled over and unwittingly exposed my naked bottom. The boys reacted with whistles and cruel laughter. Then they all ran away and there was only silence.

I pulled up my underpants and shorts as best I could and smoothed down my skirt. I was alone in the middle of the playground, with tears making erratic paths down my burning cheeks. My wild-horse pride lay trampled on the grass; I felt that I could never face anyone ever again. I hid until it was time to take the bus. All the way home I sat rolled up in a ball on the back seat without raising my head or saying a word. At my stop, I ran to the door and down the steps of the bus, entered the house and went directly to my room. When my mother announced dinner I said I wasn't feeling well and didn't want to eat.

I don't remember how I made it through the next days or how I managed to go back to class and face my friends and those boys. I only know that I never was a horse again; the freedom and joy of being an invincible, proud, and noble animal, was over. Never again did I neigh at the top of my lungs, or run at breakneck speed across the fields of the schoolyard, or of life. All that is left is a flickering memory filled with nostalgia of the days when I was a horse.

TRUTH, LIES AND OTHER INVENTIONS:
AN AUTOBIOGRAPHY

And it goes this way: confessing not to be any more saintly than my neighbors, it would not trouble me if this foolishness (which I write in such vulgar style) were to be enjoyed by all those who can find some pleasure in it, so that they may see how a person lives with so many adventures, dangers and adversities.

—Lazarillo de Tormes

A Kind of Beginning

Although quite accustomed am I to lying, you can be sure that it's God's truth when I say to you that I write these words against my will, firstly because what's herein is none of your business even though it may pique your fancy, and furthermore because much of it causes me great shame. However, I gave my word—due partly to vanity and partly to inertia—so more shameful would it be not to keep it, though by honoring it forthwith I lay myself open to vulture tongues, like a poor Prometheus bound to a modern-day rock.

Let me commence by saying that I became a liar not by choice, but rather by force, and this habit, evil as it may be, when applied to the weaving of stories and novels is not so terrible as other vices I might have acquired given the twists and turns of destiny. Of course, in regard to destiny, some are given to swearing that it can't be known, others that it does not exist and all depends on chance, and I'm not here to accuse them of bending the truth. Nonetheless, my life it is and nobody else's, and I can assure you that my destiny did exist and aware I was of it from the moment I could reason, because others created it for me and made it so solid and inevitable that all my objections were in vain. So let it be well understood that I'm not to blame for what I am, but rather certain circumstances and persons left me no choice. I, however, accuse no one of my misfortune, especially not those who have passed to a better life, and for what good they taught me I am grateful and for what ill they imparted I forgive them. And so as not to make a long story longer, I'll proceed to recount what I remember of my life and wanderings, who were my teachers, and how they led me down a path of many thistles and few delights.

Where and of Whom I Was Born

You should know straightforth that my given name is Brianda and my last name Domecq, as I am the daughter of Pedro Domecq González, native of Jerez de la Frontera, Viscount of Almocadén, Knight of Calatrava, and black sheep of his family. My mother is Elizabeth Cook Schlesinger Moëller, native of New York, and with no further distinctions beyond her beauty and composure. But, so the truth be known, I must confess to such a disorderly mixture of bloods—including French, English, Spanish, and Moorish, as well as German, Jewish, Irish and what there be of American—that I am more a stew of leftovers, with much spice and little substance, than a dish of any recognizable cuisine.

And since one's life should be told as it was and not as one would have wished it to be, I shall begin by telling you that my father, whose family had more noble lineage than money, wed my mother, whose own family had neither lineage nor money, in a second marriage against all the laws of Spain, the Holy Catholic Church, and his first wife, who could not or would not understand the romantic, adventurous spirit of the would-be knight, and therefore waited for him to settle down and return to her, their four children, the noble titles, and the properties left in Spain. When my father offered no sign that he would do so but, quite to the contrary, got a speedy divorce in Reno, Nevada, and married my mother in a civil ceremony with two strangers for witnesses, the church declared him a bigamist and thus, to my shame, I was born an illegitimate child by all civil and ecclesiastic laws from across the sea. And to this bastardly birth I was still entitled over thirty years later when the daily papers of Madrid found me for once worthy of mention. Fortunately, childhood is a distant garden, full of innocence, and far removed from the criteria and judgments of society, and my illegitimate status was unknown to me until I matured, so it carried no weight during my formative years and could not give me any more complexes than the numerous ones I created for myself.

My fortune—not always black—was such that my father, a mining engineer by obligation and a storyteller by inclination, took to novelizing life for me even before I was born. Thus my first years were spent dallying in an imaginary reality whose beginning was the greatest love story ever heard, overshadowing Romeo and Juliet, pulverizing the passion of Lady Chatterly, shaming Anna Karenina and Madame Bovary, and with, of course, a happy ending in which the enamored knight triumphs over distance, dissension, blows, insults, suspicions, and incredible obstacles to win the heart of the gorgeous, blonde, slender, flirtatious, and spoiled New York model and sweeps her off her feet, carrying her away, not to a castle in Spain but to a small apartment on 72nd Street in the big city.

To the rollercoaster story of their passion, my father added the tragicomedy of his paternity because the apple of his eye refused to get pregnant in spite of his valiant attempts. When, notwithstanding his four Spanish offspring, my mother began to doubt his virility, my father in a fit of rage, dealt such a blow to the wall so as to leave a huge hole, then wept like a child for the insult to his manhood, and straightway ushered himself off to see a doctor and prove to the world and my mother that her sterility was not his fault. The medic confirmed what everybody but my mother already knew and recommended a long vacation as a remedy. My father returned home, swept my mother up in his arms, and carried her off to London. The journey ended with the first explosions of war that sent myriad bombs descending upon the British capital. Against wind, tide, and my mother's will—which was no small matter—my father managed to pack off his beloved, as barren as she had arrived, on the last transatlantic transport leaving for New York, barely a few days before the "blitzkrieg." He stayed behind in London to live another of the numerous adventures of his life. Years later, with thundering voice and theatrical gestures, he'd recreate for me in minute detail Winston Churchill's inspired speeches, "I have nothing to offer but blood, toil, tears and sweat" and he'd wipe the sweat off his dry brow. "We shall fight on the beaches, we shall fight on the landing grounds, we shall fight in the fields and in the streets, we shall fight in the hills; we shall never surrender," and he'd shake his fist in my face. And then, adding his favorite Roosevelt quote, "We have nothing to fear but fear itself," he would hug me, swearing that he and the British had lived "their finest hour." When he returned home months later, the happy reunion after such a long separation succeeded where the vacation had failed, and I was conceived.

My birth was auspicious, although I am not sure of what. It occurred under the sign of Augustus and by the way of Julius Caesar, in a hospital on Manhattan Island on the first of August 1942, nine months after the United States entered World War II. The operation to extract me from the maternal womb saved me the trauma of a natural birth and marked my leonine character with unruliness and rebellion, two qualities that have accompanied me ever since. Resolutely positioned butt first and with the umbilical cord firmly entwined around my neck, I would have been quietly strangled before ever knowing the joys and sorrows of this world if it had not been my mother's will to sacrifice her marmoreal belly for my well-being. Whereupon her body revenged its mutilation by refusing to produce even a drop of milk, in spite of being majestically endowed to do so, and I was bottle-fed, which, according to the psychologists, explains my subsequent fondness for wine, cigarettes, and biting my fingernails.

From the moment of birth I proved the proverbial stone in my progenitors' shoe. Scarcely had they extracted me like a pea from the maternal pod, when the doctor fearfully observed that I was incomplete: Missing was the little toe on my left foot. In order to ascertain that nothing else was lacking, I was subjected to an intensive medical examination. My father, who feared the absence of some grey matter or worse, was relieved to know that the rest of me appeared to be complete and decided that one little flaw was not enough to deny me the name he had always wanted to give a daughter. Ignoring the fact that I was pale of skin, with platinum hair and blue eyes, and that I had been born in the United States during the twentieth century, Brianda was the name he bestowed upon me. The name, obviously, didn't correspond to my destiny, but rather to someone else's; nonetheless, it was imposed upon me. However, as has been said, one gets used to everything except death, and thus in spite of myself, I adjusted to the name and it to me and we have been together for more than fifty years now, through good, bad, and even worse times.

According to my father, the original Brianda for whom I was named was the wife of the valiant captain whose fate it was to defend the city of Jerez de la Frontera against the Moors. "In the bloody battle," he narrated as if he had been there, "he was mortally wounded and as he lay dying he called for his courageous followers. Brianda was at his side when he made them swear to defend Jerez with their very lives. They all signed the oath and he, taking his last breath, dipped his hands in his own blood and sealed the pact with them. Brianda lifted her husband's sword and taking the oath herself, laid it across the signed paper. From then on, she led the battle until the final victory. In recognition of her valor and that of her men, Jerez has on its coat of arms a pair of bloody hands and a crossed sword, and the Domecq family has the same but with white-gloved hands as a sign of nobility."

And so it is that having been born in the century of electric lights, telephones, television, and space travel, I carry a history and a name that are almost medieval, and my first years were spent in an imaginary and anachronistic world, full of knights-errant, renegade viscounts, finicky ladies in love, well-fought battles, unending romances, and the daily passions of my parents who, when they weren't squabbling, were making love, all of which made me undisciplined, imaginative, fiery, and bad-tempered, and taught me to live inopportunely among fantasies and dreams. I cannot claim to have suffered and obviously I have no complaints because we only hobble ourselves by criticizing our parents. Nevertheless, it's worth saying that for many years I was ill-prepared for a reality that, outside the paternal fantasies, was materialistic, consumer-oriented, practical, and opportunistic. Perhaps if I had stayed in that imaginary space that my father had woven around me, I would have been happy, but the world spins and we spin with it and soon I was to learn that outside my first home another yarn awaited me.

Sudden Changes and How We Came to Live in Paradise

I had just turned five when life took to moving on and tumbled me out of the blissful cradle of ignorance. My parents, seeing their worth increase once the war was over, decided to abandon the small apartment on 72nd Street and move to a house in the country where I would enter the realm of reason and consciousness, and where my father could realize his dream of tilling the earth himself, an occupation forbidden to Spanish noblemen. This, in the barbaric new world, was not only allowed, but actually encouraged. So we begot ourselves to an old farm in good condition with a main house, a carriage house, a wine cellar, a stable, and a barn. The nearest neighbor was four miles away and to the town of New Canaan, Connecticut, it was a half hour by car. My father declared the place Paradise, and who was I to contradict him or to know back then that all paradises have their particular serpents to ruin them.

The truth is that it did seem like paradise, surrounded as it was by flowering fields in spring, a vegetable garden that offered its bounty in summer, apple trees decorated in the fall with red temptations, and deer that came in winter for the fruit buried beneath the snow. All around there were dark woods that hid the mysteries of life and countless adventures just waiting to whet my appetite for the unruly. The house was rife with fascinating hiding places in the basement and attic, which contained passageways and secret closets where I could disappear for hours and make those enclosed spaces expand with my imagination. And thus, as the indoors grew with my fantasies, the outdoors furnished the elements that fed them: the miles and miles of forests, the myriad sights, the delicate or pungent scents, and the varied sounds of the beetles, squirrels, birds, foxes, skunks, and deer that inhabited it. Nothing could have nourished the stories of my childhood like the solitary freedom that the farm provided: It was an unending inspiration for curiosity and imagination, both of which already had been well stimulated by my father's incorrigible habit of romanticizing life.

It is not my place to point an accusing finger at my progenitor and say that if he had raised me with a little more common sense my life would have been different and I would have served, perhaps, for something more than telling lies, but I swear to you that I was born innocent as a dove and not a liar, and if there is one truth in this world it is that children learn what others teach them and little else. Furthermore, I know that once I had lost forever my childhood paradise, adjusting to other places was harder than counting hens' teeth and therefore I began fantasizing about that which was lacking, and herein lies the cause of all subsequent maladies with which my life since hath runneth over.

Nevertheless, so as not to pluck by the beard those that fed me, nor think small beer of those who gave me life, I will admit that in that paradise I gleaned one whole year of happiness before reality imposed itself. Until then there was no thunder or lightning to disturb my good fortune. Even though my parents continued to occupy the nights with ferocious fights and passionate reconciliations, the days were gloriously mine. I'd escape from the house and run to the barn, where I'd jump into the hay from the highest beam, as a bird swoops into its nest. In the stable I learned to neigh and prance about like a horse; once transformed into a spirited stallion, I galloped across the field to the edge of the woods. There I'd dismount from myself, take off my saddle, and tether myself to the trunk of a tree, so I could sneak into the shadow of the forest as a hunting dog. A sudden crackling of leaves would make me perk up my ears, stand at attention, and sniff the breeze until discovering the culprit: a squirrel! The little animal would scurry away and I'd scamper after it 'til I came upon its lair, a shallow cave that could shelter me from a storm or hide me from tigers and bears. Once the danger had passed, I'd become a valiant scout, leaving my hiding place and advancing to the chuckling, crystalline brook where I would sail my ships of leaves and twigs until reaching the clearing once more and starting all over again, inventing a new reality.

Weekends were different. My father and I novelized the days with living stories: What once was just imagined, materialized into active experience. Two against the world, we defended mother's castle from attacks by the Moors, the arrows of Indians, and assaults by bandits. Together we did not fear kings or rooks. He'd protect me and then I'd save him, arriving in the nick of time to kill an enemy. Our magic tractor transported us the world over in search of the fountain of youth, the holy grail, or the horn of plenty, which was always right where we finished plowing the vegetable garden. On foot we'd go up and down the furrows planting the seeds of illusion and cabbage, of fantasy and broccoli, of dreams and tomatoes, onions, potatoes, and strawberries so we could return home with the good news that this winter the people would not starve because we had done our day's work.

I learned everything a rightful man should learn and that was the root of the damage because instead of becoming an exemplary gentleman, I became a misguided woman. I was taught to be brave and untiring; to enjoy strong odors like the smell of sweat, skunk, or manure; to endure wounds without complaining: blackberry scratches, scrapes from falls, slivers and stickers from hay. At my father's side, I learned how to drive a tractor and a jeep, to be a hunting dog and retrieve the pigeons and ducks he shot; fearless, I climbed the apple trees to reach the reddest fruit. I mastered the art of digging up earthworms for fishing and impaling them on the hook without disgust or remorse. And since I was not lacking in cleverness, I also taught myself a few tricks to earn some money. For twenty-five cents I would pick wild berries for my mother to make jam or pies; in the forest I collected treasures—shiny stones, old bottles, acorns, and twigs with strange shapes—which I auctioned off on Sundays. My mother and father bought everything from me with laughter that revealed their complicity, and I filled my pockets with change to spend in town on the next market day. Nevertheless, unbeknownst to me, soon that magical world was going to end, never to return.

How My Paradise Was Lost

Woe is me for not appreciating all that I had until I saw it lost forever! Into my paradise came the proverbial snake; my character and life turned bitter and I began to pay for my sins even before having committed or enjoyed them. How true is the saying that the road to Hell is paved with good intentions! My parents, believing they were doing a good turn, trampled everything beautiful in my life and showed me where the shoe pinches when they decided to give me a sibling for company. I was dead set against the plan and told them so quite clearly with tears streaming down my cheeks, but they turned a deaf ear to my pleas. When they announced that the bun was in the oven, I tried to defend myself and defend what was mine and, seeing that objecting and crying did not swerve them from their dark intent, I pretended to lose my appetite. My grandmother was right when she said that you cut off your nose to spite your face and you never know what master you serve, because that offensive fast did me not one bit of good. My mother, seeing such good food going to waste and feeling the hunger of two, ate it all to the benefit of the other and my misfortune, and thus, instead of vanquishing the enemy, I helped to feed him. With the extra food, the worm inside her grew faster and, even though I tried to ignore its existence hoping it would disappear, my wretched mother kept rubbing it in my face, "Look, dear, here is your baby brother or sister. Feel how he kicks and squirms!" she would say, and I would be the one kicking and squirming, throwing such a temper tantrum that I'd be sent to bed without supper.

Skeletons began to creep out of the cracks in my world as

the hunger and rage brought on nocturnal terrors. Night after night I heard the footsteps of the bogeyman as he crept down the hallway to the door of my room. Night after night I would scare him away by crying and screaming and raising such a ruckus that my father would come running to hug me and swear there was nothing outside my door. I'd shiver with disbelief until he told me a story to help me fall asleep. Unfortunately, since I repeated the scene so many times, one evening he came and instead of a story I received such a sonorous spanking that from then on I feared my father more than the bogeyman.

Nothing managed to change reality, not the stories nor the whacks, not even the hunger strikes, and after having been queen of the roost for six years and four months, I was dethroned, and doubly wronged, for my mother gave birth to a baby boy, a bitter offense that took me many years to forgive. In order to survive, I resorted to my only remaining recourse: completely ignoring the little insect's existence, and inventing a reality in which baby brothers died at the very instant of conception. But one rotten apple ruins the whole barrel, and soon my paradise was crawling with worms. As weeks passed I had to abandon the fantasy that uninvented my brother's existence and try other means to thwart his increasing demands for attention.

I became rebellious and obstinate, learned to lie and steal things I didn't need, developed a suspicious clumsiness that made me knock over or break something at every meal, and began to wet my bed every night. My nocturnal accidents inevitably coincided with my brother's feeding time, which drove my mother half crazy since she had two children crying at the same time; she ran from one room to the other, not knowing who to care for first. One night I thought I'd won the battle when she let the baby bottle grow cold while she changed my wet sheets, but the little beast raised such a row that the following night she reversed the order and I was left for more than an hour, shivering with cold and thinking that far from finding a solution to the problem, I had worsened my fare and would soon die of pneumonia.

Between my rebellion and my brother, who was a sickly crybaby from the start, my mother's scarce patience soon wore so thin that she hired a black nanny and instructed her in our care. Things went from bad to worse. The nanny occupied the attic, blocking access to my hideaways; she was ill-tempered, strict, cared nothing for stories, and openly preferred my brother, especially when he was asleep. In such wise, I had two enemies under the same roof. The only bright omen was that the nanny drank, and more than once I saw her staggering with the feeble baby in her arms. I crossed my fingers and waited. Finally one afternoon she drank so much whiskey that her muscles went slack and she dropped the worm on his head. She was fired in a trice but, to my chagrin, the accident had no effect on the little beast's existence.

Thereafter, my rejection of the invader of paradise surpassed the limits of sibling rivalry and became plain and simple hatred, a clean and direct desire for annihilation. My imagination ripened into malice capable of creating the most cruel and sadistic tortures without blinking. With a kitchen knife, I slowly disemboweled all of my previously beloved stuffed animals and left them, one by one, under my brother's crib. One morning my only doll was found with a belt around her neck, hanging from the lamp in his room. I became surly, solitary, and prone to temper tantrums. My Eden had become Hell on earth. My mother scolded me and since I ignored her, she tattled to my father when he came home at night. He'd impose some dire punishment that for me was totally unfair, and thence would set off a tirade of shouts and cries, howls and stomps, promises to be good, mixed with accusations of neglect until my ballyhoo would manage to waken the insect who consequently joined in with his own caterwauling. Whereupon my mother would lose what little patience she had left, and begin to berate my father for having caused such an outrageous uproar. In turn, he'd flare up, blaming her for not being able to handle her own daughter, and thus our house would rock with bellows, cries, howls, and accusations until my father, fed up with the infernal racket, would whisk me up, lay me kicking and screaming across his knees, give me a vigorous spanking, and send me to bed.

All those blows to my royal buttocks convinced me that not only had the sickly crybaby taken my place, but also that I had fallen from grace due to my monstrous absence of maternal feelings toward the worm. Finding myself an outcast, I took to locking myself in my room and only coming out for meals.

How My Parents Decided to Send Me to School and the Pack of Nonsense I Learned There

My family showed very little imagination and even less impartiality when they chose to solve the problem by sending me to school; it would have been much more legitimate and educational to put my brother up for adoption. After all, I had arrived first and according to all the rules I knew, the one who gets there first, wins. But the world was upside down, and the worm was getting the early bird, instead of vice versa, and I was handed over to the first-grade teacher at the New Canaan Country Day School to see if she could mend my ways and drum some sort of reason into my wooden head.

To tell the truth, one of the few things I learned in grade school was that my father had bestowed on me no gift when he gave me a name so Spanish, exotic, and unpronounceable in a setting where everyone spoke English. How I suffered during the first week of school each year when I had to pronounce my name out loud in front of everybody! I cursed my progenitor more than once—God forgive me—for not calling me Susan or Mary or Jane. The teachers would make me repeat my name two, three, and even four times.

"Brenda?"

"No, Bri-anda."

"Ah, Brayenda!"

"No, Bri-an-da."

"All right, Miss Domequiu. . ."

In more than one class I settled for being called Brayenda Domequiu just to avoid repeating a name so at cross-purposes with the time and place where I was born. To my friends I was "Bri," which would have provoked a lot of teasing if they had known that's the name of a stinky French cheese, but some luck was with me and ignorance favored me more than any knowledge ever had.

Neither did other things learned there benefit me; rather they seemed only to contribute to my already scampish nature. There were fifteen students in the class and as soon as I entered I realized that my brother was not the only vermin that would make my life miserable: At least half of my classmates belonged to the band of the enemy and they saw me as their victim from the very first day. Because I was so blonde they called me "albino," and although I didn't know what the word meant, ignorance couldn't hide the insult, so I lashed back, calling them "pigs, brats, stupid idiots." Furthermore, my hair was fine and a bit straggly and my mother insisted on braiding it into what looked like a rat's tail; the boys didn't take long to identify it as such and to take turns yanking it whenever the teacher wasn't looking.

"Teacher! Tommy pulled my braid!"

"No, I didn't, teacher."

"Yes, you did, you stupid, dirty pig! He pulled my braid."

"I promise, teacher, I didn't do it."

"Yes, you did," and I'd swat him one. He'd grab my wrist and we were off. "Ouch! He's twisting my arm, owww!" I'd howl and kick him in the ankle. By the time the teacher reached us we were rolling in the aisle, shouting insults, hitting, pinching, kicking, and biting each other any way we could.

"Miss Domequiu! Young ladies don't behave that way!" and she'd drag me to the principal's office so that Miss Johnson could instruct me in the proper behavior for young ladies and inform me that as punishment I'd get a zero for the day and lose my recess privileges. Thus I learned that as a "lady" I had no right to defend myself, I should ignore any insult that was hurled at me, the meaning of "justice" varies according to one's sex, lies told with enough conviction are accepted as the truth, and the last thing in the world I wanted to be in life was a "lady."

I must admit that not everything was negative, although even that which seemed positive was not very useful. In workshop, for example, I made several clay animal figures and learned that I would never be an artist because my rabbits looked like cats, my horses like dogs, and my dogs like rats, but I had a good time. They also taught me how to make candles. They set a pot of liquid wax on a table and gave each of us a white cord. Then we walked single file around the table, sinking the cord in the wax each time we got to the pot. Since I was too impatient to circle the table so slowly, I butted in line and sunk my cord into the wax before the previous layer had hardened and my candles came out pitifully deformed and a yucky green color. I proudly brought them home to my mother but the first one she lit melted in seconds, leaving a gooey paste on her best tablecloth, so she threw away the rest. My fascination with the plastic arts was short lived.

What was more interesting, though it did me no good either, was to discover that the boys and girls in sixth grade hid in the coat room to kiss, and that in the boys' bathroom my classmates would compare their weenies to see whose was the longest. Among the girls it was common to compete over who had the most handsome father, and for a long time my classmates despised me for the obvious reason that mine was by far the winner. School was also where I was deprived of my dearest illusions: marrying my father, making my brother disappear, being number one, being good and loved by all. The only illusion that I never had was winning the silly stars that other kids wore on their foreheads when they behaved well. Once, by mistake, I got a bright green one; as soon as the teacher looked away I gobbled it up so no one would know. From then on I was careful not to behave well enough to merit another one. . .

The Useful Lessons I Learned at My Grandmother's House

Between the worm at home and the enemy at school, I found no consolation except on weekends when my father would take me away from my unbearable reality and lead me down the paths of fantasy. Nevertheless, the fates undoubtedly willed my undoing because a new change would take away even that minimal salvation. My father began to take business trips and every month he would go to Venezuela, Colombia, or Mexico to establish new companies. With his absence, I was as lonely and unprotected as a snail without a shell. No more stories, no more walks or games, nobody to take me hunting and fishing or to harvest the vegetables or drive the tractor. My mother had more than enough work just taking care of the crybaby, and she scarcely had time to wake me up in the morning, feed me at noon, and send me to bed at night. The strained situation intensified my rebellion and not a day passed without my throwing one or two temper tantrums, or maybe even three. If it was time to get up, I didn't want to: temper tantrum. If I was supposed to eat, I didn't like the food: temper tantrum. If it was bedtime, I wasn't sleepy: another tantrum. I understand now how deep my mother's love must have been since she did not strangle me during that tumultuous period of my life; however, it was not she who saved me, but rather my grandmother, who arrived one day at the height of one of my tantrums and announced, "This child is jealous of her brother. She needs more attention and you don't have time. I'll take her home with me for a few days."

From then on I would spend weekends, holidays, and vacations at her house. She didn't play with me or tell me stories or make up fantasies, but she talked of life and living, and there I learned everything that school couldn't teach me and that has helped me make a way for myself.

My grandmother's house was very feminine; everything was pink—the walls, sofa, curtain—and full of celestial beings: statues of cherubs, lamps with little angels, seraphim hanging on the walls and painted on ashtrays where my grandfather left his burned-out cigar. She herself, on the other hand, was not at all "feminine;" she had a strong, solid character and without much ado always managed to impose her will on everyone. Her opinion, expressed in a straightforward and definitive manner, was many times contradictory but never subject to doubt. She had a passion for collecting antiques and almost all her furniture had been bought with monthly installments of five or ten dollars at the antique stores on Second Avenue. They were acquisitions of love and I believe she worshipped them more than she did my grandfather, because every time she decided to move—a very frequent occurrence that generally came about without warning—she'd not lose sight of a single piece of furniture until it was carefully accommodated in the new home, but for her spouse she just left a note on the door of the old house with the new address.

It was obvious who ran the household. Short, slightly plump, and cuddly but not fat, she never doubted herself: She dictated what would be done, what should be done, and that is what was done. One day when my grandfather treated himself to a luxury car, she didn't let him into the house until he returned it and retrieved their old one and the cash he so foolheartedly spent. It was one thing to invest in antiques, but throwing away money on a fancy car was a totally different matter.

My grandmother's mother lived with them for many years and my grandfather had an ongoing battle with her. Very early on in their marriage, my grandfather had dared to draw an ultimatum, "Either she goes," he said, referring to his mother-in-law, "or I do."

"Well then, you go," my grandmother answered, "and don't ever forget: I might not like her either, but she's my mother and it's my duty to take care of her until she dies."

My grandfather, who was no fool, tucked his tail between

his legs, so to speak, because he understood then that for his wife duty was stronger than love and eventually he would end up losing.

My grandmother dyed her hair auburn to cover the grey and painted her fingernails bright red. I never saw a grey hair on her head or a broken nail on her hands in spite of the fact that she did all of the housework. Once a week she went to the beauty parlor to have her hair washed and styled and her nails done. At night she used a hairnet to preserve her hairdo for the following seven days. She bought her summer clothes in the winter and her winter clothes in the summer to take advantage of the seasonal sales. This wasn't due to stinginess or avarice, as she explained, but rather because she had suffered great poverty as a child. When, in the Crash of '29, my grandfather lost almost all his savings by speculating in the stock market, she took the financial reins of the house and from then on he turned over his monthly check and received an "allowance" to play poker with his friends on Fridays. "Greed is the root of all evil," she told me in order to make clear the difference between her need to take care of their money and the extreme avarice that produced world wars and family breakdowns.

Although she spoke in aphorisms and often contradicted herself, for the first time I felt understood in my desolation and abandonment. "Misery loves company" proved to be true for me, because talking with her alleviated a lot of the anger that I carried inside. Thus I felt close to her as she told me about her life, so similar, in my childish opinion, to mine. Her father had died and mine had abandoned me; her mother, instead of remarrying and forming a new family, had taken up with a married man with whom she had a secret affair for twenty years: a traitor, just like my mother who had taken up with the baby brother. They were so poor that they had to move in with an aunt, just like I had taken shelter in my grandmother's house, looking for consolation. The only thing I didn't understand or agree with was that she considered it a tragedy to have been an only child, without brothers or sisters, while I believed that that would have been my salvation. No matter how much I argued that solitude is not alleviated by a sibling, she refused to concur. "Loneliness is a cancer," she repeated, and never budged from that judgment.

Since grandmother wasn't exactly bound by the truth, she never bothered to explain to me some of the maxims that seemed to rule her life. She pronounced them and left me to put them in context, which I did to the best of my meager abilities. From her I learned that the worst sin is to waste food in a hungry world. "Waste not, want not," she would say when I left something on my plate, and she would wait until I ate the last pea. "Happiness is for fools," she explained when somebody spoke of happiness, insinuating that it was better to be intelligent and unhappy. "Bringing children into this world is selfish," she affirmed, leaving me with the idea that parents have children for their own pleasure and not for the benefit of their offspring. Often she contradicted herself, declaring on the one hand, "Love has disappeared from this world," as if something very important had been lost and on the other hand, "Love is for the birds," as if only fools believed in it. Nevertheless, even when she contradicted herself, I kept accommodating those maxims next to my worries and anger to use as directions in life. She even spoke to me about social issues. "If I were president," she said in regard to the population explosion, "I would put a machine with sterilizing rays on every corner in order to 'fix' any man who walked by so he couldn't have any more children." "Men are no good," she said, meaning—as I figured out later on—that her own husband was no good because he had turned out to be a drunk, a philanderer, and a gambler. On the other hand, she adored my father and believed that my mother didn't deserve him because "women are devious; you can't trust them," an affirmation from which, obviously, she and I were excluded. As I listened to her, a whole new panorama opened up for me, a real world in which one should have definite opinions and irrefutable judgments in order to avoid being contaminated by doing the wrong thing.

Her favorite topic was religion. She was an atheist ("thank God," she said) because of a humiliation she had suffered as a child. While living at her aunt's house she was forced to wear her cousins' hand-me-downs. That in itself wasn't so bad, "waste not, want not," she'd say, but when she had to wear an old coat on which they had sewn sleeves of a different color to go to church, that was the last straw. At that moment she knew that God did not exist, because if He had existed He never would have permitted such humiliation of a little child. From then on she was an atheist; more than an atheist: a zealot of atheism, because not a day of her life passed without her mentioning God in order to deny His existence.

I took to all of these lessons like a fish to water. I never again left anything on my plate because by eating it all I could save the world from hunger: I had a reason for being. And my unhappiness did also, since being unhappy meant being intelligent, and being intelligent was much more interesting than being happy. Her solution to the population problem seemed like an excellent idea, although a bit late because that sterilizing machine should have been invented before my brother's birth; and as for God, if an old coat was enough to justify my grandmother's denial of Him, then surely my heartwrenching loss of Paradise would do the same for me.

With my grandmother I felt sure of myself, mature, and determined; in her house I only remember throwing one temper tantrum. I cannot remember the motive, but I was in the living room stomping and screaming and she was in the kitchen. When I realized she was ignoring me, my anger became pure rage and I began to kick all the antiques in the house. That she continued ignoring this outrageous provocation was more than I could stand, so I wiped off my face, went to the kitchen, and planted myself in front of her.

"Didn't you see what I just did?" I challenged.

"No. I didn't see anything. What did you do?" she asked, continuing to stir the stew.

"I kicked all your furniture."

"Really?" she said without changing her tone. "That makes me very sad because I take good care of my furniture. Why did you do that?"

The rage had wiped out my memory of why I had done it, and suddenly I felt very badly. I hugged her and promised never to do it again. Then she took me by the hand, led me to the living room and asked me which piece of furniture had been kicked the hardest. I pointed to an antique magazine rack next to the easy chair. She emptied it, turned it upside down and wrote on the bottom with blue ink: "When I die I want my granddaughter Brianda to have this rack," and she signed it.

"Now, come with me to the kitchen and while I finish dinner you can tell me a story."

I don't remember what I told her but it was very long, involved, and full of fantasy. When I finished she was enthralled.

"You are going to be a writer," she announced, without bothering to explain what that was or whether it was good or bad, and the next day she gave me my first notebook and a new pencil with a sharp point. That day I began to write and I discovered my life's direction and the refuge that somehow has allowed me to survive.

I would have liked to have continued visiting my grandmother; in fact, I would have liked to have lived with her. However, as she would say, the world spins around many times and the spin that mine was about to take would change my destiny completely.

How the World Spins with the Help of Martinis

On one of those rare nights when I let down my guard and agreed to go to bed early, my bad luck took advantage and became even worse, and therein I discovered how small a matter it takes to ruin one's life.

Upon arriving home from the office, my father was so pleased with the peace and quiet that reigned, both children being asleep and my mother contentedly preparing dinner, that he decided to celebrate with a martini. He prepared two well-served drinks and while they were sipping them he told my mother the news. The business in Mexico was going so well (that was the good news) that next year he would have to spend more than six months south of the border (that was the bad news). While they were contemplating what to do to save the unity of the family, my father prepared another couple of martinis and they tipped their elbows once more. There is no doubt that wine makes a poor counselor because after the second drink my mother mustered all the courage in her slender body and proffered up a solution that was convenient for them but disastrous for my formative years: They decided to move to Mexico. My adverse destiny kept me asleep that evening and, like an unsuspecting feather, I was swept along by the breeze of misfortune without my being able to protest or even declare that I wanted to live with my grandmother. Furthermore, since they'd had two martinis each, in order to balance things out they made another disastrous decision for me. They agreed to send me to a summer camp in order to distance me from my grandmother's influence since her nonsense, according to them, was making me obstinate and spoiled. Innocent me! I did not find out about the first decision until months later, but the next day I was informed of the second one.

All protests, tears, and tantrums were in vain, and around mid-July they packed my things, put me in the car, and took me to a place in Maine far away from civilization. There my parents unloaded my suitcase, gave me a kiss, and left me with a group of boys and girls more or less my age. I was terrified and wanted to go home, but it was too late: The automobile was already disappearing down the highway as fast as possible. I closed my mouth so as not to cry, for if I had opened it the howl that was stuck in my throat might have escaped. The group nearby interpreted my silence as snobbishness and ignored me in turn. It was like being in the vicinity of a pack of miniature gorillas. Already one of the boys had established himself as the dominant male and was entertaining everybody by spouting what seemed like a lot of nonsense to me, but it made the rest laugh. Upon realizing that I wasn't impressed, he approached and looked me straight in the eye. I sustained his gaze even though a chill ran down my spine as I recalled the many torments I had endured from his kind in school.

"Gentlemen prefer blondes," he said sarcastically, referring to my corn-colored hair, "fortunately, I'm not a gentleman."

He turned around and went back to the group, laughing at his own wit. I forgot that I didn't want to talk to anyone and opened my mouth.

"The world goes 'round many times," I muttered with a

dry voice, remembering my grandmother's lessons, "while I sit on my porch and wait for my enemy's funeral procession to pass by."

Nobody understood a word of what I said, that was clear, but the laughter stopped. When the counselor called us to dinner, they ran off; I followed slowly. Since I was the last in line almost all the food was gone and I had to settle for some tasteless vegetables. Summer had started out poorly and threatened to get worse. The surprises didn't end there. Back then the theories of a man named Dewey were in vogue; he preached that children's morbid curiosity about sex was due to repression and covering things up. Therefore, according to him, we should uncover everything, especially the body. With this taboo eliminated and their curiosity satisfied, children would forget about sex until the appropriate time and they would grow up healthy and optimistic. He apparently hadn't read Freud. Following Dewey's advice, my parents, who had been raised in the Victorian manner, had decided to liberate me from the traumas of a repressive education—which couldn't have been very severe, judging by their passionate encounters —by sending me to a modern, progressive Auntie-Mame style camp that boasted of promoting the latest ideas in education. I have no doubt that their intentions were good, but as my grandmother would say, the road to hell is paved with good intentions, and sometimes when parents try to save their children from their own hang-ups, they actually leave them not only hung up, but twisting in the wind.

After dinner we went to the cabin that would be our dormitory. Since there were no divisions, it was obvious that we were all going to sleep together. There were twenty bunks; the girls were assigned to the lower beds and the boys to the upper ones (perhaps so that in the future we would not doubt who would be on top and who would be on the bottom). I took the bed nearest the door so I could escape if necessary and, to my surprise, the dominant male chose the one above mine.

"I still don't like blondes," he said, so that I wouldn't get any funny ideas.

"And I don't like conceited dopes," I replied.

Once the beds were distributed, the counselor announced that we had five minutes to put on our pajamas and get ready to sleep. Everyone started giggling, but he was dead serious.

"Whoever is not ready in five minutes receives a demerit and won't be able to swim tomorrow."

That night forty sheets were transformed into frolicking ghosts as we all struggled to undress under the covers amid giggles and blushes. I ended up with my pajama on inside out but I was saved from being seen once more without underpants. I swore that from then on I would go to the bathroom to change. Little did I suspect what awaited me.

The following morning there was no escape. After breakfast it was time to swim and we all headed to the lake with bathing suits, caps, and towels in our hands. There was a small cabin that served as a changing house for everyone. The counselor once more announced that we had a few minutes to change and whoever left their underwear on under their suits would not get to swim. There was no doubt: We were all meant to see each other. There was a moment of absolute silence and then the boys, less shy and more eager to spy on us than to hide from our sight, began to undress as fast as they could. We girls tried to defend ourselves with our towels as we peeled off our clothes and leapt into our suits, but it was more than impossible and in a little while we had all seen what we had and what they had, and there was nothing more to hide. Needless to say, after the first day bodies lost their mystery and we undressed in front of each other as naturally as eating pie.

One might think that Dewey had triumphed over Freud and our "morbid" curiosity had disappeared, leaving us pure, healthy, and able to share an innocent and asexual cohabitation. Far from it. Curiosity didn't disappear, it only mutated, and having been satisfied in regard to the construction of the opposite sex, we then wanted to know just how those different parts functioned. From curiosity love is born and in a few days the dominant male confessed to me that he really did like blondes, I replied that I liked him, too, and holding hands, we went off into the woods to experiment with kisses and hugs, which was all that our nine years of age allowed us. From then on we were inseparable; we did everything together and invited no one to join us. We ate together, slept together (he in the top bunk, and I in the bottom one), swam, and went for walks together. We chose the same clay and carpentry workshops; during our free time—when we weren't hiding and kissing—we devoted ourselves to constructing entire towns of miniature cabins made of twigs that fell from the pine trees, creating roads and fences around them, and inventing stories that set them to life. We learned to row in the lake, to fish using tiny frogs as bait, to plow the vegetable garden, to clean the stables and groom the horses, to play baseball, and to climb the highest trees. I would have wanted that summer to last forever: I loved and was loved in return. I felt like nothing was missing; that sweet existence with freedom and company was the height of happiness, but like everything in life—except fantasies—the summer came to an end and so did our days at camp. Parents arrived to pick up their children and mine, with the insensitivity they often have shown in regard to childhood needs, not only wrenched me away from the happiness of my first love, but also had the bad taste to bring along my little brother. In the hustle and confusion of departure I lost track of my first boyfriend, and we didn't even get to say goodbye to each other. In revenge, I pinched my brother as soon as we got into the car and, watching him cry, I endured my desire to do the same.

How My Roots Dried Up When We Moved

Sometimes it seems as if life despises us and adverse fortune is ready to put us to the test each time we start feeling secure and think we're headed in the right direction. Sometimes it's not even temptation or sin that makes us lose our way, but our parents' eagerness to do what is right for us. Rather than leave me half-orphaned during the following years, my parents chose to pull me up by my roots, which were quite tender back then, and transplant me not only to another country, but also to a different culture, another language, another reality. At the time, I didn't even realize the damage they were doing, although to tell the truth it would not have done a bit of good anyway, since my parents, like most, were ill-disposed to take my opinions into consideration. Children are trusting and unaware, and tend to go where they are sent without putting up much of a fuss. Thus, after camp when I arrived home and it was unrecognizable with all the decorations in boxes, clothes in suitcases, and furniture piled up for the move, I didn't panic as I should have, but simply asked where we were going. I was informed that we were moving to Mexico, but not that Mexico was three thousand miles from my grandmother's house, everybody spoke Spanish there, children were left in the care of maids while mothers went to play golf or cards, and fathers became workaholics and rarely had time to play with their daughters. In short, they didn't tell me that my life was going to be so different that even I wouldn't recognize it. They just said we were going to Mexico, and I was as unsuspecting as ever.

A few days before the trip they invited my uncle, aunt, and cousins over for a farewell reunion. The eldest cousin and I were the same age and we usually shared more rivalry and envy than friendship. At that time collecting trading cards was the rage. Like playing cards but without numbers, they were sold in packages of ten and had a wide variety of beautiful pictures on the back. There were always repetitions from one pack to another to keep the trading and the sales going. An individual's value was measured by the size of his or her collection and the competition was fierce and unscrupulous: Anything—theft, lies, extortion—was justifiable in order to get more cards. I had managed to collect about two hundred, including a series of horses, dogs, cats, wild animals, flowers, landscapes, and historical figures, all in beautiful, colored photographs printed on the cards, and I was proudly waiting to show them to my cousin.

The day of the reunion he arrived carrying a small black suitcase and we immediately went up to my room to negotiate the trading. When he opened the suitcase I couldn't believe what I saw: It was full to the brim.

"How many do you have?" I asked, disheartened.

"More than a thousand. There are more than one hundred and fifty just of horses. Do you want to trade?"

With a sigh I took out the twenty cards for which I had doubles, and passed them over to him in exchange for more than a hundred that he handed me. I didn't have hardly any of his doubles; I waited while he looked mine over and checked to see if he had them. When he finished, he had found only two of mine that he didn't have. Carefully I chose one of his cards with a white horse and was just about to choose another when he said, "That one's worth two; it's really hard to get. If that's the one you want, I'll keep these two of yours."

"That's not fair."

"Then choose two others: The white horse I'll only trade for two."

I gave in; I wanted the horse. Once the trade was made he began to show me his whole collection, one by one, bragging about the ones that were most difficult to find and that I surely never would have. I was dying of envy. I had never desired anything so much as that magnificent collection; I really coveted it, but there was no way: My cousin was so stingy that even when he had three copies of a card, he wouldn't give me one. When they finally called us to dinner, I breathed a sigh of relief and ran downstairs. Afterwards we played hide-and-seek and other foolish games until my aunt and uncle announced their departure. They were in a hurry to leave before nightfall and my cousin got into the car without saying goodbye. As soon as I returned to the house I discovered his oversight: There was the suitcase, next to the door. I picked it up and ran to the barn to hide it without even thinking about how I was going to finagle keeping it. The next day my cousin called and I pretended to know nothing.

"Suitcase? What suitcase? Oh, I don't remember. Mom, my cousin wants to know if you found a black suitcase," I shouted. "No, my mom says that you didn't leave it here, but I'll look for it and if I find it I'll call you."

I hung up. There were three days remaining until we left for Mexico, and I was suddenly in a great hurry. There I could become the queen of trading cards, without having to cover up anything. Every so often I would go to the barn to adore my treasure, caught up in greed in spite of my grandmother's lessons; over and over again I counted the cards and the hours left before our departure. When the day arrived, I retrieved the ill-begotten windfall, placed it on my lap and for the whole trip didn't let it out of my sight for fear that someone would do to me what I had done to my cousin. I was so busy taking care of my free pass to power and glory that I didn't even notice when they pulled me up by the roots and transplanted me to a garden so foreign that instead of having an incredible advantage I was actually at a terrible disadvantage: I didn't speak the language, I didn't know anybody, no one had ever heard of the famous trading cards, and I found myself completely destitute of Royal Crown Cola bottlecaps, which were the currency of exchange among the youngsters of my new country.

My first roots dried up and I didn't grow new ones. I lost all notion of my identity and allowed myself to be pulled back and forth like the shuttle on a loom, from here to there and back again, without grasping onto anything, not even my own life. I learned to speak Spanish in the kitchen, to smoke cigarettes at school, and to kiss the neighbor boy on the back terrace of my house. The only remnant of my other life was the notebook in which I wrote down the things that happened to me, composed love poems to the boyfriend of the moment, made up stories to tell myself since my father was too busy with his new business to bother, and complained bitterly about my troubles to nobody in particular. I would have liked to think that with all that solitude and suffering I was being punished for my unfortunate heist, but I didn't have even that satisfaction. I was intelligent enough to realize that it would have been the same with or without the theft. The notebook filled up with laments and sorrows, and the trading cards were forgotten and eventually lost.

If it's true that in this life you pay for your sins, my parents must have been deep in debt to have deserved such a daughter as myself. With no ties, I drifted around aimlessly, like a leaf in the wind, without purpose, doing what I wished or whatever displeased them. I sought out the worst company and was more of an accomplice than a friend to anybody. A defiant tomboy, I accepted any challenge to climb the highest tree, throw eggs at parked cars, or write bad words on the walls. When they sent me to bed, I locked my bedroom door and climbed out the window to go to some cohort's house. Two days a week I missed the school bus because I was off buying *jícamas* dusted with chili pepper and lime, outside the schoolyard fence. In class I did only enough to pass, took cheatsheets to the exams, or brazenly copied my classmates' answers. I smoked on the sly and, when my parents went on vacation, had parties at home without permission or ransacked their closet to put on my mother's best dress and go to the movies with some friends. I was worse than the plague and there was no punishment or scolding that could deter me. The only positive thing I did, if you call stringing together a series of lies and fantasies something positive, was write. The first notebook was followed by others that filled up with verses and nonsense. When asked to write an essay in school, I negotiated for writing fiction and thus began to produce my first short stories. They were unbelievable and melodramatic, like the one about the boy in Leonardo da Vinci's time who constructed the first version of a model airplane and actually flew it, running after it, until he and the small apparatus fell into quicksand and disappeared, leaving no proof of his invention. When I finished the story I cried for the tragic fate of my protagonist but never bothered to find out if there was quicksand in Italy.

My father, trying to improve my culture, my intellect, and my manners, urged me to read, and I obliged but not as he would have wished. Far from reading edifying texts, I sought the books he bought on trips and hid on the top shelf of the closet, works full of sex and violence that served to round out my bad education. By the time I was fifteen an all-out war had been established between my parents and me, and they were losing. To remedy the situation, they sent me away to Massachusetts.

I don't resent their putting me in a boarding school. I think I spent the best two years of my life there. Without the distraction of boys, I began to take an interest in my studies. There I produced my first poems and stories that deserved recognition by a teacher; there I decided that some day I would write a book, or several. During semester breaks or on long weekends I would go to my grandmother's house, where I recaptured much of what had been lost. My grandmother and I would talk about politics, social problems, the women's liberation movement, sex ("Everything changes when sex raises its ugly head"), and my various and sundry boyfriends. However, that sheltered and stimulating existence was just as fictitious as the fantasies I enjoyed with my father in New Canaan and far from solving my uprootedness, I ended up convinced that I was divided between two worlds and didn't belong to either. While studying in the United States, I lost contact with Mexico; when I visited my parents, I lost contact with my friends in New England. Still feeling like the shuttle on a loom, I spun back and forth across the threads without becoming part of the fabric. My only certainty lay in my grandmother's prediction, "You are going to be a writer some day," and I dedicated my free time to filling the pages of my notebooks with nonsense.

Nevertheless, my parents wanted the best for me and for themselves, too, and since both desires were realized by keeping me as far away from home as possible, they demanded that

I continue my studies in a prestigious college in the United States. Accepted by one in New York, I moved to the big city. There is no greater solitude than that of a sprawling metropolis and, even though I was enjoying my studies more and more ever since I had decided to be a writer and they began to make sense, my spirit was headed a hundred miles an hour toward a crisis: The feeling of not belonging anywhere—and thus not advancing toward anything—exacerbated the usual existential angst of adolescence, and at the end of the second semester I gave up on college, my studies, the big city, and visits to my grandmother's house, and came running home to my parents to take refuge from myself and life in general.

The decision was made and there was no power in the world that could change my mind: I would not go back to New York. During the next few years I devoted myself to finding some roots to replace those lost in the early transplant, grasping at any crumb of culture that passed my way. I started studying social work and became aware of a Mexico I hadn't known previously, full of hunger, disease, and social injustice. In my dreams I saw myself as a savior of the poor and oppressed and, armed with a little theory and a lot of goodwill, I began to visit the city's ghettoes in search of wrongs to set right. In spite of my goodwill, I was obviously not cut out for that job. While attempting to do concrete good and not just create fantasies, I found myself more helped by those in need than they by me, since when they saw I was so blonde, blue-eyed, and white-skinned, they put themselves at my service. By trying to give them something, I ended up taking from them the little they had so as not to offend them when they invited me into their homes and offered me their precious tortillas and beans.

I returned home with the double guilt of having eaten and not having helped, so I gave up social work. From that experience, however, I did acquire a good friend, a Dominican nun.

Since I observed she was intelligent and not drugged by the "opium of the masses" as my grandmother called it, I began to think that maybe my parents had done me a poor favor by neglecting to provide me with a religion to hold onto during existential crises and I even felt sorry for my grandmother who, tending to be dogmatic, had chosen atheism instead of the religion that was suddenly being offered to me.

I was in an extremely mystical trance, with daily mass and communion three times a week, when I met the man who would become my first husband. To my parents' relief, he distracted me from the path toward sainthood and put me on the road to passion, so even though I continued to take communion every Friday, I did so only after a long confession of all the erotic transgressions he and I had committed during the week. At the end of a year we got married and the confessions were no longer necessary, although I admit that love is never so passionate as when it is a sin committed in secrecy. A short time after getting married I abandoned my assumed religion, which, without the stimulus of sainthood or sin, was full of stifling trivialities. My son was born within a year and my daughter three years later and, finding myself anchored to home, I decided to return to writing. I registered for a correspondence course through the "Famous Writer's School" in the United States and began to devote myself to my professional formation. I learned a lot of tricks of the trade but the substance evaded me, and I realized that, once again, I was hindered by my lack of roots. I was living immersed in the culture of Mexico, but trying to write in English about situations in the United States, for North American readers. Thereupon, I cut the only umbilical cord that connected me to my country of origin: I stopped thinking, speaking, reading, and writing in English, and went after the mastery of new tools of the trade.

As neither organization nor logic has ever been my forte, I

pursued my new goal in the usual haphazard way, taking advantage of whatever opportunity presented itself. The first thing that crossed my path was a job in the publications department of the Olympic Games Organizing Committee. Even though I didn't learn to write while there, I did meet many young Mexican writers who entered the office as if it were their home, talking about the student movement and water polo, repression and the pentathlon, politics and horsemanship, the takeover at the University and diving competitions, the massacre at Tlatelolco and track events. I learned about Mexican punctuality when I saw the luxurious programs released after the events so nobody bought them; about writers when I noticed they were more interested in the tequila my boss kept in her drawer than in finishing their work; about politics when several revolutionary intellectuals showed up for work wearing conservative suits and having shaved off their leftist beards, after the police occupied the National University.

Subsequent to the Olympics and the student movement, I went down the Mexican road of nepotism and asked a friend of my father for a job as a creative writer in her advertising agency. There I polished my art of short fiction by writing ads for Corona beer for the bullfight aficionados, Delicado cigarettes for boxing fans, the General Gas Company for the general public, and other products whose dubious qualities I sought to enhance in order to write better material. I did get a lot of experience, although I am not sure that it was all beneficial. However, I enjoyed advertising because among other things, I could see the product of my efforts in a short time, in contrast to the literary world in which waiting periods are interminable and sometimes fruitless. But that work would not last long because during my absence my household shuddered to a halt and when the maid went back to her home town, I had to quit my job and return to the odious tasks pertaining to my sex: cleaning, making beds, preparing meals, and taking care of children. In my free time—that is, for ten minutes before falling asleep—I kept writing in my notebook, now in Spanish so I would not lose what little ability I had acquired.

Things were going from terrible to even worse, and when I realized I was becoming embittered, I decided to seek work I could do at home. So as not to deviate from my chosen path, I decided to do translations, and set out to find a project to get me started. Luck would have it that a publisher took pity on me and in less than a week I had my first job. It was definitely not literary, but it was educational: A pamphlet on venereal diseases (back when the threat of AIDS had not appeared and the sex-related diseases were the simple, domesticated ones that we always knew about) and thus I found out about cankers and lesions and other wonderful things produced by licentious practices, knowledge that perhaps would serve in the future for writing horror stories. There is no doubt something is learned from every experience in this life.

From my second translation, however, I confess that I didn't learn about much more than the profound structural differences between English and Spanish. They gave me *The Ford Manual for Mechanics* to translate. It was an unwieldy book of about a thousand pages that described every part of an automobile down to its last screw and I had to convert that technical labyrinth from English to Spanish without making the paragraphs longer! Thus I learned that in English it is perfectly fine to put six or seven adjectives before a noun, such as "the backseat, left window, short knobbed fastening screw" which in Spanish became the length of an entire litany to the Virgin Mary. The result was neither English nor Spanish and by the second year they decided that the mechanics understood the manual better in the original language than in my translations and I lost that job which, even though boring, paid very well. Thereafter, I set my sights higher and sought literary translations by visiting a prestigious publishing house whose director told me that for the moment there were no translations, with the exception of one very long and difficult text which he himself was doing. It was the most recent work by Norman Mailer, *Of a Fire on the Moon,* about the Apollo 11 flight. Thoroughly discouraged, I went home and continued translating pamphlets for veterinarians and warmed-over articles in English for national magazines. Six months later they called me from the same publishing house I had visited previously to say they had a translation for me to do, but like everything in this country, it was "due yesterday."

I raced over there, recognized Mailer's enormous 600-page manuscript and listened to the director, who had obviously decided not to translate it, asking me to finish the work in a month. I negotiated six weeks, convincing him of my absolute seriousness in regard to such tasks and then went home to shut myself off from civilization. I worked eighteen hours a day: the household crumbled and my head ached, not to mention my rear end, but I managed to finish just in time. It seemed like a good translation to me. I gave instructions to the editor to revise only the syntax but without changing the meaning because what was said in English, I had said in Spanish. I sat down to wait, believing that this work placed me on the threshold of my literary career.

The truth is that all sins are paid for somehow and a few of mine must have slipped by unpunished so that my first "literary" work turned out so poorly for me. The director ignored my instructions and turned over the manuscript to a copyeditor with two grave defects: First, she didn't speak English and second, she didn't speak Spanish either, because otherwise I can't explain how she could produce sentences that made absolutely no sense in either language. I especially remember going into a state of shock when I arrived at a sentence that had cost me a lot of work and which, in my opinion, had turned out quite well. Mailer described the people who were waiting to see the blast-off of the rocket headed to the moon: "They awaited the dawn with a shot of red-eye in the glass," which I managed to translate into understandable Spanish without betraying the southern jargon. When I arrived at the page where the sentence was I found the copyeditor had rewritten the sentence so, in Spanish, it now read something like: "They awaited the dawn with red eyes behind shot pieces of glass." Tears streamed down my face like the long-lost shot of red-eye when I saw that my budding literary career was going down the drain of incompetence like so many other good things in this country. I closed the book without reading another word; I shall never know how many or what kind of changes were made because I don't intend to subject myself to such a masochistic task. The book is hidden in a drawer of my library, a painful monument to frustrated hopes and so much blood, sweat, and tears that have been washed down the sewer by a bureaucracy that intrudes on even the best of ventures.

Needless to say I abandoned translations and seriously thought about giving up being a writer when the world took another turn, this time in my favor. My first husband's business began to prosper and it was no longer necessary for me to earn my share of our expenses; at the same time, my youngest child entered school and I was left with my mornings free. Even though I was thirty and felt much too old for schooling, I swallowed my pride and registered for classes at the National Autonomous University of Mexico, commencing a course of studies that would teach me the profession to which I aspired. It was just a beginning, but the great sorrows I had endured in my life had taught me to be a hard-working and law-abiding woman, no longer twisted, because since then I have had no master and no love other than writing, unless you count the children with whom I have been greatly blessed.

And the rest is mostly well known, so it would be useless to recount it.

And all I have to say for those who would criticize the length or the content of this writing, its veracity or mendacity, I only will add that not everything that happened is told here, nor did everything happen that is here told, since a long time ago I gave up distinguishing between truth and fiction because all truth made memory and words is fiction, and, after all, life is not a dream but a story, and the important thing is to tell it or, as my friend Lazarillo de Tormes said, "I believe it to be beneficial to have such remarkable and incredible things brought to the attention of so many, since perchance someone may read about them and find something that edifies him, and those who do not delve so deeply will find some entertainment. . .because if it were not so, very few would write for themselves, since it takes quite a bit of effort. . ." and I, in order to end well by cozying up to the classics, say the same.

BIBLIOGRAPHY

Book-length Fiction, Essays, and Works edited by Brianda Domecq

Acechando al unicornio: la virginidad en la literatura mexicana. Mexico City: Fondo de Cultura Económica, 1988. Anthology.* written by Brianda Domecq.

A través de los ojos de ella. Mexico City: Editorial Ariadne, 1992, 2 volumes. Anthology of stories by Mexican women writers, edited and with analysis by Brianda Domecq.

Brianda Domecq: De cuerpo entero. Mexico City: Ediciones Corunda, 1991. Autobiography. Translated in this volume as "Truth, Lies and Other Inventions: An Autobiography." Reprinted in Spanish in Domecq, Brianda, ed. *Mujeres que cuentan (Siete escritoras mexicanas de su puño y letra)*. Mexico City: Ediciones Ariadne, 2000.

Bestiario doméstico. Mexico City: Fondo de Cultura Económica, 1992. All stories included in this volume.

La insólita historia de la Santa de Cabora. Mexico City: Planeta, 1990. Translated by Kay S. García, as *The Astonishing Story of the Saint of Cabora*. Tempe, Arizona: Bilingual Review Press, 1998.

Mujer que publica, mujer pública. Mexico City: Diana, 1994. Essays by Brianda Domecq about Mexican women writers.

Once días . . . y algo más. Mexico City: HARLA, 1991. Novel. First published in 1979 by Universidad Veracruzana. Translated by Kay S. García as *Eleven Days,* Albuquerque: University of New Mexico Press, 1995.

*Introduction and edited by BriandaDomecq.

Un día fui caballo. Mexico City: Biblioteca del Instituto de Seguridad y Servicios Sociales de los Trabajadores del Estado, 2000. Stories. Some included in this volume.

Voces y rostros del Bravo. Mexico City: Editorial Jilguero, 1987. Book-length essay.

Works about/including Brianda Domecq

Agosín, Marjorie, and Nancy Abraham Hall, eds. *A Necklace of Words: Short Fiction by Mexican Women*. Fredonia, NY: White Pine Press, 1999.

Bados-Ciria, Concepción. "Historia/s y texto/s en *La insólita historia de la Santa de Cabora,* de Brianda Domecq." *Revista de Literatura Mexicana Contemporánea 1.2* (1996): 80–85.

De Beer, Gabriella. *Contemporary Mexican Women Writers: Five Voices*. Austin: University of Texas Press, 1997.

Diccionario de Escritores Mexicanos, Vol. II. Mexico City: Instituto de Investigaciones Filológicas de la Universidad Autónoma de México, 1988. 46–49.

Finnegan, Nuala. "Reproducing the Monstrous Nation: A Note on Pregnancy and Motherhood in the Fiction of Rosario Castellanos, Brianda Domecq, and Angeles Mastretta." *Modern Language Review 96.4* (2001): 1006–1015.

García, Kay S. *Broken Bars: New Perspectives from Mexican Women Writers*. Albuquerque: University of New Mexico Press, 1994.

López González, Aralia. "La huella de lo reprimido: fisuras y suturas." *Signos: Anuario de humanidades 5.1* (1991): 239–48.

Merithew, Charlene. *Re-Presenting the Nation: Contemporary Mexican Women Writers.* New Orleans: University Press of the South, 2001.

Pérez de Mendiola, Marina. "La insólita historia de la Santa de Cabora," From *The Location of Memory to Demystification. Gender and Identity Formation in Contemporary Mexican Literature.* New York and London: Garland Publishing Inc., 1998. 53–85.

Shaw, Deborah. "Las posibilidades de la escritura femenina: *La insólita historia de la Santa de Cabora,* de Brianda Domecq." *Literatura Mexicana 10.1–2* (1999): 281–312.

Strand, Cheryl. "Conversation with Brianda Domecq." *Bilingual Review 23.3* (1998): 248–254.

Reviews in English of Brianda Domecq's novels

The Astonishing Story of the Saint of Cabora: Multicultural Review. March 1999: 58. *UC Mexus News.* Summer 1999: 23. *Hispanic.* July/August 1998: 94. *Library Journal.* 15 June 1998: 105. *Booklist.* 15 May 1998: 1594. *Kirkus Reviews.* 15 May 1998: 691. *Publishers Weekly.* 27 April 1998: 46.

Eleven Days: New York Review of Books. 20 April 1995: 39.*Feminist Bookstore News.* May/June 1995: 115.